APPLICATIONS OF MACHINE LEARNING IN POWER ELECTRONICS FOR INTEGRATION OF RENEWABLE ENERGY SOURCES

INTELLIGENT ALGORITHMS FOR EFFICIENT ENERGY INTEGRATION

DR. KUMAR K
DR. V LAKSHMI DEVI

Made with ♥ on the Notion Press Platform
www.notionpress.com

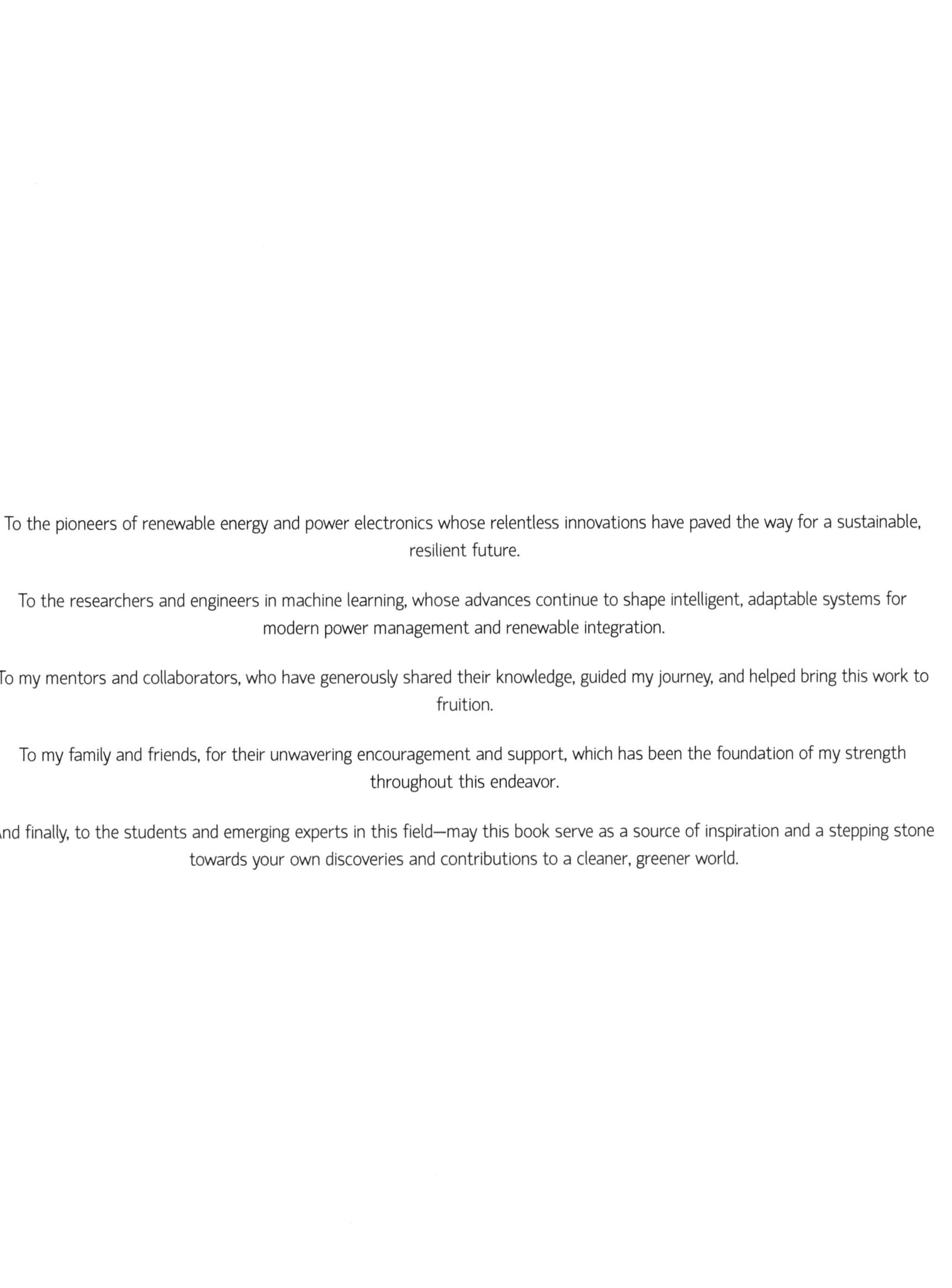

To the pioneers of renewable energy and power electronics whose relentless innovations have paved the way for a sustainable, resilient future.

To the researchers and engineers in machine learning, whose advances continue to shape intelligent, adaptable systems for modern power management and renewable integration.

To my mentors and collaborators, who have generously shared their knowledge, guided my journey, and helped bring this work to fruition.

To my family and friends, for their unwavering encouragement and support, which has been the foundation of my strength throughout this endeavor.

And finally, to the students and emerging experts in this field—may this book serve as a source of inspiration and a stepping stone towards your own discoveries and contributions to a cleaner, greener world.

Contents

Foreword *vii*

Preface *ix*

Acknowledgements *xi*

Prologue *xiii*

1. Introduction To Power Electronics And Renewable Energy Integration 1
2. Fundamentals Of Machine Learning 6
3. Electronic Converters For Renewable Energy 10
4. Machine Learning For Power Converter Control 15
5. Machine Learning For Predictive Maintenance In Power Electronics 20
6. Forecasting And Scheduling Of Renewable Energy Using Machine Learning 23
7. Fault Detection And Diagnosis In Renewable Energy Systems 29
8. Optimization Of Renewable Energy Integration With Machine Learning 34
9. Power Quality Improvement In Renewable Systems Using Machine Learning 39
10. Hybrid Machine Learning Models For Power Electronics 43
11. AI-Driven Energy Management Systems 47
12. Emerging Trends In Machine Learning For Power Electronics 51
13. Case Studies And Real-World Applications 54
14. Future Directions And Challenges 57

Foreword

The fusion of renewable energy sources with power electronics represents a fundamental shift in modern energy systems. As the global focus sharpens on sustainable energy solutions, machine learning emerges as a critical tool for advancing the efficiency, reliability, and resilience of power electronics. This book, Applications of Machine Learning in Power Electronics for Integration of Renewable Energy Sources, addresses the opportunities and challenges at this intersection, providing a comprehensive overview of how artificial intelligence and machine learning methodologies are reshaping the landscape of renewable energy systems.

Authored with a focus on both theoretical foundations and practical applications, this work serves as a valuable resource for engineers, researchers, and students exploring the rapidly evolving field of smart energy. By delving into advanced techniques for control, predictive maintenance, and system optimization, the book equips readers with the knowledge needed to innovate and drive progress in sustainable power technologies.

This contribution is timely, bridging the current knowledge gaps and opening new avenues for integrating renewable energy into global infrastructure. It is my hope that this book will inspire further exploration and implementation of these transformative technologies, fostering a future where clean energy and intelligent systems converge for the betterment of all.

Preface

The integration of renewable energy sources into power systems has become crucial in the global pursuit of a sustainable, eco-friendly future. However, this transition poses unique challenges, particularly in maintaining power quality, ensuring system reliability, and efficiently managing energy flow. As the field of power electronics evolves, the adoption of machine learning techniques has emerged as a transformative solution to address these challenges, offering unprecedented insights and optimization opportunities.

In writing Applications of Machine Learning in Power Electronics for Integration of Renewable Energy Sources, my goal has been to bridge the fields of machine learning and power electronics, particularly in the context of renewable energy systems. This book explores the practical applications and transformative potential of machine learning for power electronic systems, enabling renewable energy to become more stable, predictable, and efficient. Through these chapters, readers will encounter foundational knowledge, case studies, and emerging trends that highlight how machine learning is reshaping power converter control, predictive maintenance, fault detection, and energy forecasting within renewable systems.

I hope this book serves as a valuable resource for engineers, researchers, and students navigating the intricate and evolving field of renewable energy integration. It is my sincere wish that readers will find both inspiration and practical guidance to advance their work and contribute to a more sustainable energy future.

Acknowledgements

I would like to express my heartfelt gratitude to everyone who supported me in the completion of this book, Applications of Machine Learning in Power Electronics for Integration of Renewable Energy Sources. This journey would not have been possible without the help of several individuals and institutions.

First and foremost, I extend my sincere thanks to my mentors and colleagues whose expertise in the fields of power electronics and machine learning inspired and guided me throughout the research and writing process. Their invaluable insights enriched the quality and depth of this work.

I am also deeply grateful to my family and friends for their unwavering encouragement, patience, and understanding during the long hours spent on this project. Their continuous support motivated me to push through challenges and stay focused on my goal.

Finally, I would like to acknowledge the contributions of researchers and authors whose pioneering work in renewable energy integration and machine learning applications laid the groundwork for this book. Their achievements serve as both a foundation and a source of inspiration.

Thank you all for your invaluable support.

Prologue

The transformative journey of renewable energy has only just begun. As nations strive toward a future of sustainable energy, innovations in power electronics and machine learning emerge as the vital forces driving this shift. This book explores the intersections of these dynamic fields, offering insights into how machine learning models can revolutionize power electronics, making renewable energy systems more efficient, adaptable, and resilient.

With rapid advancements in artificial intelligence, machine learning is uniquely positioned to resolve complex control, maintenance, and optimization challenges within renewable power infrastructures. In this prologue, we delve into the motivation behind exploring machine learning applications in power electronics, seeking to shed light on how these technologies can support the seamless integration of renewable energy sources, making them not just viable but indispensable.

This book aims to equip readers with both theoretical foundations and practical applications, ensuring a comprehensive understanding of how machine learning techniques can be employed to tackle the intricate needs of modern power systems. As we embark on this exploration, the pages that follow will unveil a roadmap to harnessing AI-driven solutions that bring us closer to a cleaner, smarter, and more sustainable energy future.

CHAPTER ONE

Introduction to Power Electronics and Renewable Energy Integration

1.1 Integration

In power systems, integration involves the seamless combination of various components, such as power generation sources (renewable or traditional), power electronics, control systems, and energy storage solutions. The growing complexity of the power grid, with decentralized energy sources, renewable power, and electric vehicles (EVs), demands an integrated approach.

- **Challenges**: Integrating renewable energy with conventional grids presents unique challenges. Renewable energy sources are intermittent and often unpredictable, requiring advanced control systems to balance supply and demand.
- **Future Trends**: Technologies like smart grids and advanced energy management systems (EMS) are emerging as solutions for efficient integration. These systems use sensors, real-time data, and automation to improve the reliability, security, and efficiency of the power grid.

Effective integration minimizes energy losses, ensures optimal utilization of renewable sources, and enhances the overall resilience of power systems

1.2 Overview of Power Electronics

Power electronics is a branch of engineering that deals with the conversion, control, and conditioning of electrical power. It plays a critical role in both industrial and consumer applications, especially in the context of renewable energy systems, electric vehicles, and modern smart grids.

Key Functions of Power Electronics:

1. **Energy Conversion**: Power electronics devices manage the conversion of electrical energy from one form to another. This includes AC to DC conversion (rectification), DC to AC (inversion), and DC to DC conversion (voltage regulation). For instance:

    - **AC/DC Converters**: Found in solar inverters that convert DC from solar panels into usable AC power for homes or grid applications.
    - **DC/DC Converters**: Crucial in EVs for managing battery voltage levels and ensuring efficient power transfer to the drivetrain.

2. **Power Conditioning**: Power electronics are used to condition power by stabilizing voltage levels, improving power quality, and managing harmonics. In grid applications, this prevents issues such as voltage sags, swells, and

flicker.

3. **Switching and Control**: Modern power electronics utilize high-speed semiconductor devices, such as Insulated Gate Bipolar Transistors (IGBTs) and Metal-Oxide-Semiconductor Field-Effect Transistors (MOSFETs), for efficient switching and control. These enable rapid changes in voltage or current without significant energy loss.

Applications in Renewable Energy:

- **Solar PV Systems**: Power electronics in solar photovoltaic systems are used in maximum power point tracking (MPPT) controllers, ensuring optimal power extraction from solar panels.
- **Wind Energy Systems:** In wind turbines, power electronics convert variable frequency AC power generated by wind into stable grid-compatible AC power.

Applications in Electric Vehicles:

- Power electronics manage the flow of energy between the battery, motor, and external charging stations. In EVs, inverters convert DC from the battery to AC for the electric motor.
- Regenerative braking systems utilize power electronics to capture energy from braking and convert it back to the battery for storage.

1.3 Importance of Renewable Energy Integration

Renewable energy integration is the process of effectively incorporating renewable energy sources like solar, wind, and hydropower into the power grid. This is critical in ensuring that renewable energy becomes a stable and reliable component of the global energy

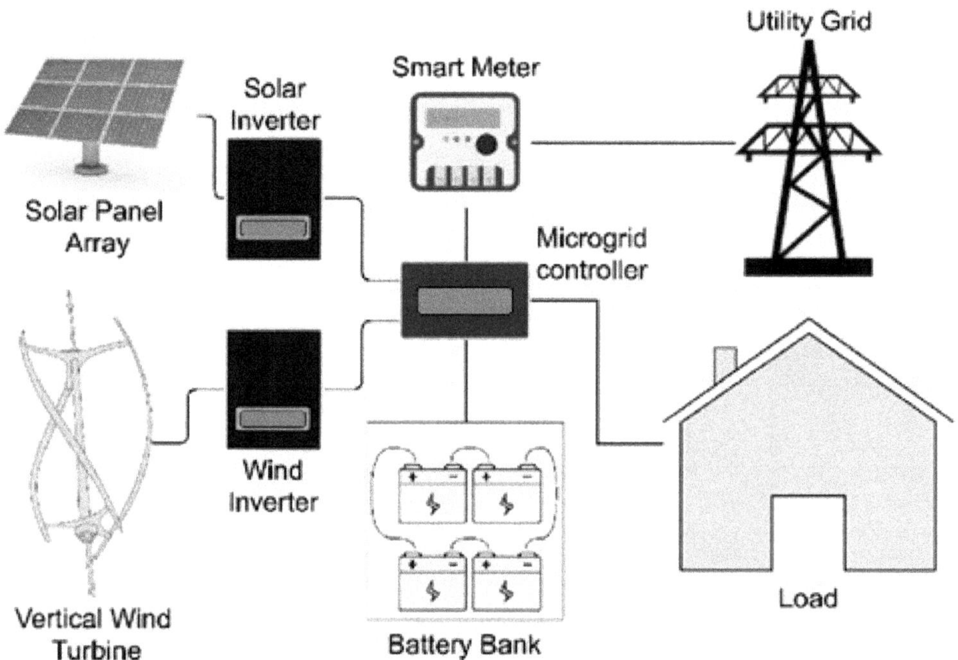

Fig .1 Schematic diagram of the grid-connected hybrid energy system

Significance of Renewable Energy:

Renewable energy integration is pivotal for reducing greenhouse gas emissions and combating climate change. As renewable sources become a larger part of the global energy landscape, effective integration is essential for stabilizing power grids and ensuring continuous energy supply.

Key Considerations:

1. **Intermittency**: Solar and wind energy are highly intermittent due to their dependence on weather conditions. Solar power is available only during the day, and wind energy generation depends on wind speed and direction. This intermittency introduces challenges for grid stability, as traditional grids are designed for continuous power from conventional sources like coal or natural gas.
2. **Grid Flexibility**: To accommodate the variability of renewable energy, power grids must be highly flexible. This is achieved through demand response strategies, where power consumption is adjusted based on supply conditions, and through the use of energy storage systems like batteries that store excess renewable energy during peak production times for later use.
3. **Energy Storage Systems**: Battery energy storage systems (BESS) play a crucial role in integrating renewable energy. They smooth out the supply of renewable energy by storing excess energy and releasing it when production dips, ensuring a steady power supply to the grid.
4. **Smart Grid Technology**: Smart grids enhance renewable energy integration by using real-time data, communication networks, and automation to optimize energy distribution. These grids can predict and react to changes in supply and demand quickly, improving energy efficiency and reliability.

01 **Intermittency and Variability**

Unpredictable natural resources cause power supply fluctuations, complicating energy management.

02 **Grid Stability and Reliability**

Voltage and frequency fluctuations from RES require advanced management and real time monitoring.

03 **Energy Storage**

Effective storage solutions (batteries, supercapacitors) are needed, but high costs and limited lifespans remain issues.

04 **Infrastructure and Investment**

Upgrading grid infrastructure for RES is costly and requires government support.

05 **Regulatory and Market Challenges**

Policies and incentives must catch up to support RES integration and ensure fair market conditions.

Fig 2 Challenges in RES integration into smart grids.

Economic and Environmental Impact:

By integrating renewable energy effectively, we can significantly reduce reliance on fossil fuels, lower carbon footprints, and create a more sustainable and resilient energy infrastructure. This shift also promotes energy independence, reducing the need for importing fossil fuels in many countries.

1.4 Role of Machine Learning in Modern Power Systems

Machine Learning (ML) is revolutionizing the way modern power systems operate by enabling predictive analytics, automation, and optimization. Power systems are increasingly complex, and ML helps handle this complexity by learning from historical data and making real-time adjustments.

Key Areas Where ML Contributes:

1. **Predictive Maintenance**: ML algorithms can analyze large datasets from sensors and other monitoring systems to predict the likelihood of equipment failures. This allows utilities to schedule maintenance proactively, reducing downtime and avoiding costly breakdowns. For instance:
   - In transformers, ML can predict overheating or insulation degradation, preventing catastrophic failures.
   - In EV charging stations, ML can monitor battery health and infrastructure stress to optimize charging cycles and detect issues early.
2. **Load Forecasting**: Power systems must always maintain a balance between energy generation and consumption. Accurate load forecasting is critical to achieving this. ML models use historical load data, weather patterns, economic indicators, and even consumer behavior to predict energy demand.
   - For example, during hot summer days, ML models can predict spikes in electricity demand for air conditioning and adjust generation accordingly.
   - Load forecasting also allows for efficient scheduling of power plants and reduces energy waste.
3. **Renewable Energy Forecasting**: ML is also crucial for forecasting the production levels of renewable energy sources like solar and wind. For instance:
   - Solar energy production is highly dependent on cloud cover, temperature, and time of day. ML models can predict future solar output by analyzing meteorological data, improving grid stability and energy planning.
   - Wind farms benefit from ML algorithms that forecast wind speeds and direction, allowing operators to adjust turbine settings for optimal energy capture.
4. **Smart Grids and Energy Optimization**: Smart grids use real-time data to make decisions about energy distribution, consumption, and storage. ML algorithms can analyze data from sensors and smart meters to optimize the flow of energy in the grid.
   - **Demand Response**: ML can automatically adjust power consumption in real-time by controlling smart appliances, EV charging, and industrial equipment, shifting load based on supply conditions.
   - **Energy Trading**: ML facilitates peer-to-peer energy trading by predicting surplus generation from distributed energy resources (DERs) like rooftop solar panels. This ensures energy is bought and sold at optimal times.
5. **Battery Management Systems (BMS)**: ML plays a critical role in extending battery life and improving performance in EVs and renewable energy storage systems. By analyzing factors like charging/discharging cycles, temperature, and usage patterns, ML models can optimize battery charging protocols, reducing wear and extending battery longevity.
   - In grid-scale storage systems, ML optimizes when to charge and discharge batteries based on energy demand, market prices, and the availability of renewable energy.

CHAPTER TWO

Fundamentals of Machine Learning

2.1 Introduction to Machine Learning Concepts

Machine Learning (ML) is a subset of artificial intelligence (AI) that enables systems to learn from data and improve performance without explicit programming. By using large datasets and complex algorithms, ML systems identify patterns, make predictions, and refine their operations based on feedback.

The core idea of machine learning revolves around the following principles:

- **Data-Driven Approach**: Instead of relying on rule-based logic, ML systems process vast amounts of data to detect patterns and relationships that might not be immediately apparent.
- **Learning from Experience**: ML models are trained using data and can improve their accuracy over time by updating their internal representations based on new information.
- **Automation**: Machine learning automates tasks that typically require human intelligence, such as recognizing images, predicting trends, or making real-time decisions.
- **Adaptability**: These systems can adapt to new and changing environments. For example, an ML algorithm predicting energy demand can automatically adjust its parameters when new factors, such as weather or time of day, are introduced.

Applications of machine learning span across various industries, from healthcare to finance, and more recently, it has made significant strides in power electronics and energy management.

2.2 Supervised, Unsupervised, and Reinforcement Learning

Machine learning is divided into three major types based on how learning occurs:

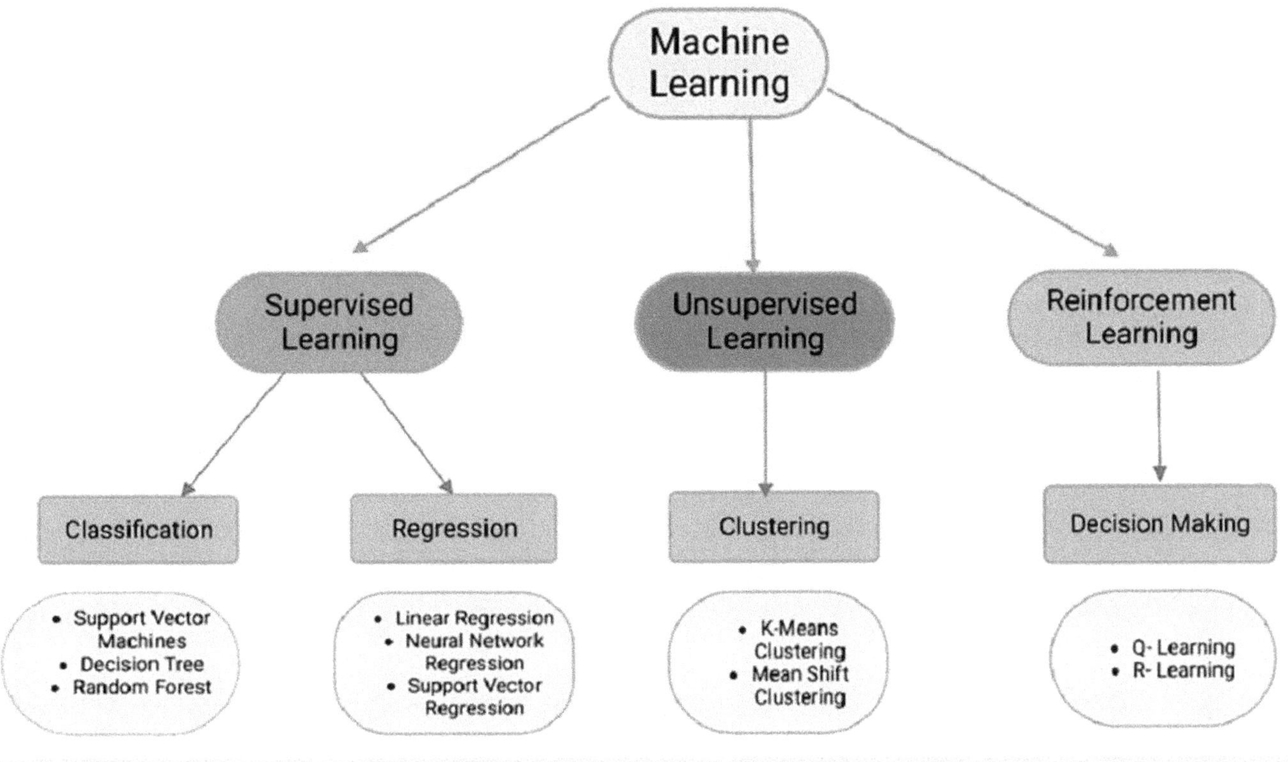

Fig.3 Types of Machine Learning:

A. **Supervised Learning**

Supervised learning is the most common type of machine learning where the model is trained on labeled data. In this context, "labeled" means that the input data is paired with the correct output. The goal of the model is to learn the mapping from inputs to outputs and use this knowledge to make predictions on new, unseen data.

- **How It Works**: During training, the model is provided with examples of input-output pairs (e.g., sensor readings and corresponding power consumption levels). The model uses this data to learn and minimize the error between its predictions and the actual outputs.
- **Applications in Power Systems**: Supervised learning is used in load forecasting, fault detection, and predictive maintenance of power equipment. For example, an algorithm trained on historical energy consumption data can predict future demand.
- **Common Algorithms**:

1. **Linear Regression**: Predicts continuous values (e.g., predicting energy consumption based on temperature).
2. **Decision Trees**: Used for classification tasks (e.g., classifying whether a power system component is healthy or faulty).

A. **Unsupervised Learning**

Unsupervised learning deals with unlabeled data, meaning the algorithm must learn the underlying structure of the data without explicit guidance. The system discovers patterns, groupings, or relationships within the dataset.

- **How It Works:** The algorithm looks for patterns, such as clusters or associations, within the data. For example, it might group different types of consumer energy usage profiles based on consumption patterns without any predefined labels.
- **Applications in Power Systems:** Unsupervised learning is commonly used in anomaly detection (e.g., identifying abnormal power usage patterns in smart grids) and clustering energy consumers based on their consumption habits for better demand-side management.
- **Common Algorithms:**
    - **K-Means Clustering:** Groups similar data points together (e.g., clustering homes based on their electricity usage profiles).
    - **Principal Component Analysis (PCA):** Reduces the dimensionality of data for better visualization and understanding (e.g., reducing the number of factors in complex power system datasets).

C. **Reinforcement Learning**

Reinforcement learning (RL) is an advanced type of machine learning where an agent learns by interacting with its environment and receiving feedback in the form of rewards or penalties. The agent aims to maximize its cumulative reward by learning the best actions to take in different situations.

- **How It Works:** The agent observes the environment, takes actions, and learns from the outcomes of those actions. The system improves its performance over time by exploring different strategies and exploiting the best-known strategies.
- **Applications in Power Systems:** RL is used in energy management systems, such as optimizing power distribution in smart grids or controlling battery storage systems in electric vehicles. For example, an RL algorithm can learn how to efficiently charge and discharge batteries in response to fluctuating electricity prices or renewable energy supply.
- **Common Algorithms:**
    - **Q-Learning:** A popular algorithm for learning the value of taking a particular action in a given state, often used for grid management and resource optimization.
    - **Deep Reinforcement Learning:** Combines deep learning with reinforcement learning to handle complex tasks, such as managing energy flows in smart cities.

2.3 Key Algorithms Relevant to Power Electronics

Machine learning has become highly relevant in power electronics due to its ability to optimize performance, improve efficiency, and enable predictive maintenance. Several algorithms are particularly useful in this context:

1. **Linear Regression**

- **Purpose:** Linear regression is a basic yet powerful algorithm for modeling relationships between variables. It's often used when the goal is to predict a continuous value, such as energy consumption, based on one or more input features (e.g., temperature, time of day).
- **Relevance to Power Electronics:** In power electronics, linear regression can be used for tasks like predicting the lifespan of components based on operational conditions or modeling the impact of voltage changes on system performance.

2. **Support Vector Machines (SVM)**

- **Purpose:** SVMs are powerful classifiers used for binary and multi-class classification tasks. The algorithm works by finding a hyperplane that best separates different classes in the feature space.
- **Relevance to Power Electronics:** In power electronics, SVMs can be used for fault classification and detection in transformers, converters, and other critical components. For example, an SVM can classify whether a power converter is operating normally or experiencing a fault based on sensor data.

3. **Decision Trees and Random Forests**

- **Purpose:** Decision trees break down data by making decisions based on input features, leading to an outcome (i.e., classification or regression). Random forests are an ensemble method that builds multiple decision trees to improve accuracy and robustness.
- **Relevance to Power Electronics:** Decision trees and random forests are often used in diagnostic systems for power electronics. For instance, they can help in detecting faults in inverters or converters, based on various operational parameters.

4. **K-Means Clustering**

- **Purpose:** K-Means is an unsupervised learning algorithm used to group data points into clusters based on their similarity. It works by partitioning the dataset into a predefined number of clusters and assigning each data point to the nearest cluster centroid.
- **Relevance to Power Electronics:** In power electronics, K-Means clustering can help identify patterns in operational data, such as grouping similar usage profiles in energy consumption or discovering different operational modes of an inverter or converter.

5. **Neural Networks and Deep Learning**

- **Purpose:** Neural networks, particularly deep learning models, are capable of modeling complex non-linear relationships. They consist of layers of interconnected neurons that process and transform input data to produce the desired output.
- **Relevance to Power Electronics:** Neural networks are used in power electronics for tasks such as predictive maintenance and system control. For example, deep learning can predict failures in power electronics devices, such as converters or inverters, based on historical sensor data, or optimize energy flows in renewable energy systems.

Reinforcement Learning Algorithms (Q-Learning)

- **Purpose:** Q-Learning is a reinforcement learning algorithm used to find the best actions in a given environment by maximizing the expected cumulative reward over time.
- **Relevance to Power Electronics:** Reinforcement learning, particularly Q-Learning, can optimize the operation of complex systems such as microgrids or energy storage systems. For example, it can learn the best strategies for charging and discharging batteries based on energy prices, renewable generation, and grid demand.

CHAPTER THREE

Electronic Converters for Renewable Energy

3.1 Types of Converters

Converters are essential in renewable energy systems, facilitating the transformation of electrical power between different forms (AC to DC, DC to AC, or adjusting voltage levels). This allows seamless integration of renewable energy sources with the power grid and other energy-consuming devices.

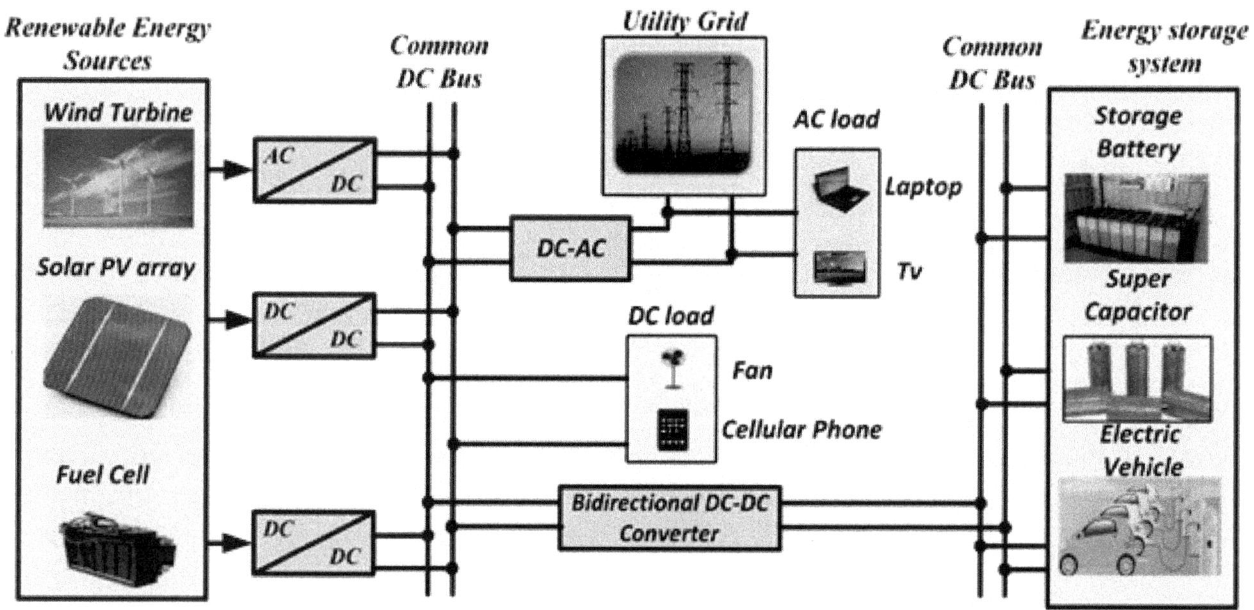

FIG .4 electronic converters in a renewable energy system.

AC/DC Converters (Rectifiers)

AC/DC converters, also known as rectifiers, convert alternating current (AC) into direct current (DC). This type of conversion is essential because many renewable energy systems (such as wind turbines) generate AC power, while others (such as solar photovoltaic (PV) systems) produce DC power, and most storage devices (like batteries) store energy in DC form.

- **Types of Rectifiers:**

- **Uncontrolled Rectifiers:** Diode-based rectifiers that convert AC to DC without any control over the output. These are simple and inexpensive but have limited functionality.
- **Controlled Rectifiers:** These use thyristors or transistors to control the amount of AC converted to DC. Controlled rectifiers allow for adjustable output and are more flexible for applications requiring variable voltage control.

- **Applications:**

  - **Solar Power Systems:** Convert DC from solar panels into grid-compatible AC using inverters. However, during storage or direct use in DC applications, rectifiers may be necessary.
  - **Wind Energy:** Wind turbines often use AC generators; rectifiers are used to convert this to DC for storage or transmission.

DC/DC Converters

DC/DC converters are devices that convert a source of direct current (DC) from one voltage level to another. This type of conversion is essential in renewable energy systems to step up (boost) or step down (buck) voltage levels to match the needs of the system.

- **Types of DC/DC Converters:**

  - **Buck Converters:** Reduce the input voltage to a lower, more usable output voltage. These are typically used in solar PV systems to regulate voltage from the panels.
  - **Boost Converters:** Increase the input voltage to a higher output voltage, making it useful in situations where the available voltage from a renewable energy source is lower than needed.
  - **Buck-Boost Converters:** Can either step up or step down the voltage, making them highly flexible in managing varying voltage levels in renewable energy applications.

- **Applications:**

  - **Battery Storage Systems:** DC/DC converters regulate the voltage between batteries and other components in energy storage systems, ensuring efficient charging and discharging.
  - **Electric Vehicles (EVs):** Converters manage the transfer of energy between the battery and the motor in EVs, ensuring optimal performance at varying speeds and loads.

DC/AC Converters (Inverters)

DC/AC converters, commonly known as inverters, convert direct current (DC) into alternating current (AC). This is critical for renewable energy systems like solar and battery storage, where DC power must be converted to AC to be compatible with grid systems or for use in household appliances.

- **Types of Inverters:**

  - **Grid-Tied Inverters:** Designed to synchronize with the utility grid, these inverters match the frequency and voltage of the grid to feed power back into it.
  - **Off-Grid Inverters:** Used in standalone systems (like remote solar installations), off-grid inverters convert DC to AC for local use, often in conjunction with battery storage.
  - **Hybrid Inverters:** Can switch between grid-tied and off-grid modes, offering flexibility in systems that combine solar, storage, and grid connectivity.

- **Applications**:
  - **Solar PV Systems**: Convert the DC output from solar panels into AC for household or grid use.
  - **Battery Storage Systems**: Manage the conversion of stored DC energy into AC for use in homes or industries.

3.2 Control Techniques in Power Electronics

In renewable energy systems, the control of power electronic converters is crucial for ensuring efficient energy conversion, stable operation, and system reliability. Power electronic systems require advanced control techniques to manage varying input conditions (such as fluctuating wind or solar irradiance) and maintain output stability.

Pulse Width Modulation (PWM)

Pulse Width Modulation (PWM) is one of the most widely used control techniques in power electronics. It works by modulating the width of pulses in a signal to control the output voltage or current.

- **How it Works**: PWM controls the amount of power delivered to the load by switching devices (such as transistors) on and off at high frequencies. By adjusting the duration of the "on" periods (the pulse width), the average power delivered to the load can be controlled.
- **Application in Renewable Energy**: PWM is used in inverters and DC/DC converters to regulate voltage levels, improve power quality, and increase energy efficiency in solar inverters and wind turbine systems.

Maximum Power Point Tracking (MPPT)

Maximum Power Point Tracking (MPPT) is a control technique specifically used in solar PV systems to maximize the power output from solar panels. Since the power output of a solar panel varies with sunlight and temperature, MPPT algorithms continuously adjust the operating point of the system to extract the maximum possible power at any given time.

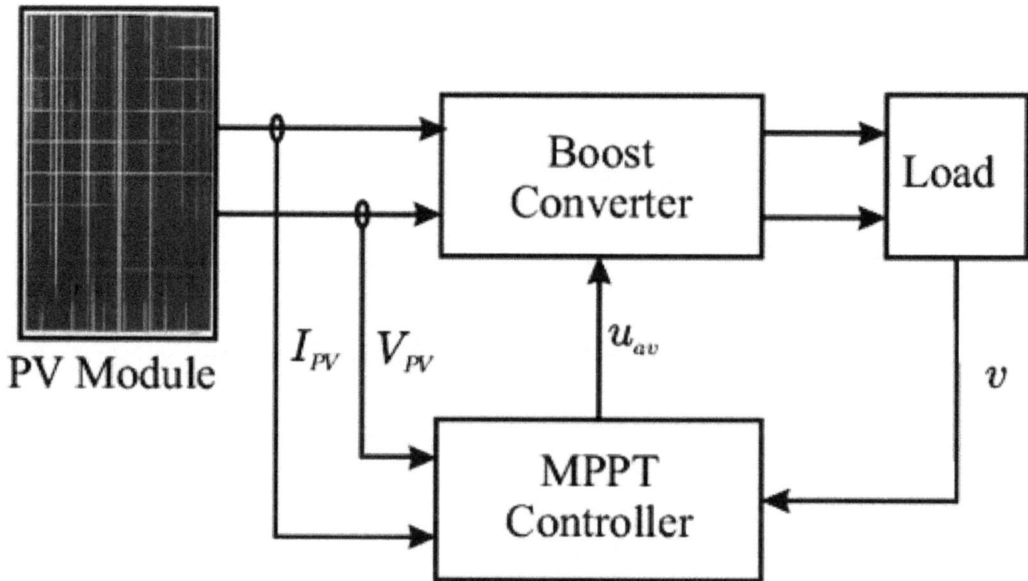

Fig .5 Photovoltaic (PV) system under a Maximum Power Point Tracking (MPPT) controller.

- **How it Works:** MPPT controllers use algorithms (such as perturb and observe or incremental conductance) to adjust the voltage or current to ensure that the solar panel operates at its optimal power point, where maximum energy can be harvested.
- **Application:** MPPT is commonly used in solar charge controllers and inverters to optimize the power generation of solar PV arrays, ensuring maximum energy conversion efficiency.

Voltage and Frequency Control

In renewable energy systems connected to the grid, maintaining stable voltage and frequency is essential to ensure grid stability and avoid disruptions. Power electronic converters equipped with voltage and frequency control techniques help stabilize the output in the face of variable input power from renewable sources.

- **How it Works:** Voltage control involves adjusting the output of power electronic converters to match the grid voltage or the voltage requirements of the load. Frequency control maintains the AC frequency (usually 50 Hz or 60 Hz) to ensure compatibility with the grid.
- **Application:** Wind and solar inverters, particularly in grid-tied systems, use voltage and frequency control to ensure that the power injected into the grid is synchronized and within acceptable limits.

3.3 Challenges in Renewable Energy Integration with Power Electronics

The integration of renewable energy sources into the power grid is critical for transitioning towards cleaner energy systems. However, this integration presents several challenges, particularly in the context of power electronics.

Intermittency of Renewable Energy

Renewable energy sources like solar and wind are inherently intermittent and unpredictable. Solar power depends on sunlight, while wind power depends on wind conditions. These fluctuations pose significant challenges for grid stability and power quality.

- **Impact on Power Electronics:** Power electronic converters must be able to handle sudden changes in input power and output stable electricity to the grid or load. Advanced control techniques (such as MPPT and voltage/frequency regulation) help mitigate the effects of intermittency, but further innovations are needed for fully reliable integration.

Power Quality Issues

The variability in renewable energy sources can lead to power quality problems such as voltage sags, swells, harmonic distortion, and frequency deviations. These issues can affect the performance of sensitive electronic equipment and reduce the overall efficiency of the power system.

- **Impact on Power Electronics:** Power electronics devices, especially inverters, must be designed with advanced filtering and control mechanisms to manage power quality issues. This includes using harmonic filters, reactive power compensation, and voltage regulation techniques.

Grid Synchronization

Renewable energy systems, especially those connected to the utility grid, must synchronize with the grid's voltage, frequency, and phase to ensure smooth integration. Any mismatch can lead to instability and operational issues.

- **Impact on Power Electronics:** Inverters and converters used in grid-tied systems require precise control to synchronize with the grid. Achieving this is particularly challenging when dealing with highly variable renewable sources. Sophisticated control algorithms are used to ensure seamless grid connection.

Energy Storage and Management

Energy storage systems (such as batteries) are crucial for mitigating the intermittency of renewable energy sources. However, managing the charge and discharge cycles of batteries and ensuring their longevity while integrating with renewable sources presents a challenge.

- **Impact on Power Electronics**: Power electronic converters play a crucial role in managing energy storage systems, particularly in efficiently charging and discharging batteries. Bidirectional converters (which allow energy flow in both directions) are commonly used in these systems. Efficient management of energy flow between renewable sources, storage, and the grid requires advanced control strategies.

Cost and Efficiency

The deployment of power electronics in renewable energy systems adds to the overall cost, which can be a barrier to widespread adoption, particularly in developing regions. In addition, power electronics devices can introduce energy losses, reducing overall system efficiency.

- **Impact on Power Electronics**: Developing cost-effective and highly efficient power electronic devices is an ongoing challenge. New materials (such as wide-bandgap semiconductors like silicon carbide and gallium nitride) are being explored to improve efficiency and reduce losses, but they are still relatively expensive.

CHAPTER FOUR

Machine Learning for Power Converter Control

4.1 Data-Driven Control Strategies for Power Converters

Power converters are essential components in renewable energy systems, where they manage the conversion and flow of electrical power between different formats (e.g., AC to DC, DC to AC). Traditional control methods rely on deterministic models of system dynamics, but as power systems become more complex, data-driven approaches—powered by machine learning—are gaining prominence.

What Are Data-Driven Control Strategies?

Data-driven control strategies do not rely solely on pre-defined physical models but instead learn from data to control system behavior. In the context of power converters, data-driven approaches leverage large amounts of operational data to optimize control actions, predict system states, and handle uncertainties or unknown dynamics that arise in renewable energy systems.

- **How It Works:**
    - Data is collected from sensors, power converters, and grid systems over time.
    - Machine learning models are trained on this data to capture the relationship between various input parameters (e.g., voltage, current, temperature) and output variables (e.g., efficiency, power output).
    - These models then adjust control signals in real-time, ensuring optimal operation even when system conditions change or are uncertain.
- **Advantages:**
    - **Adaptability:** Data-driven control strategies can adapt to changing system dynamics without needing a complete understanding of the underlying physics.
    - **Efficiency:** These strategies improve system efficiency by optimizing control decisions based on real-world data.
    - **Fault Detection:** Data-driven models can detect early signs of faults or inefficiencies by recognizing patterns in operational data.
- **Applications in Power Converters:**
    - **Dynamic Load Management:** Automatically adjusting the power converter settings to match the fluctuating load in renewable energy systems.
    - **Fault Diagnosis:** Identifying and correcting abnormalities in converter operation by learning from historical data of normal and faulty conditions.

4.2 Use of Neural Networks and Reinforcement Learning for Control

Neural networks and reinforcement learning (RL) are two machine learning techniques with significant potential for controlling power converters in renewable energy systems.

Neural Networks for Control

Neural networks are powerful tools capable of modeling highly complex, non-linear relationships between inputs and outputs. In power converter control, they can predict and optimize system performance in real-time, even when dealing with variable and noisy data.

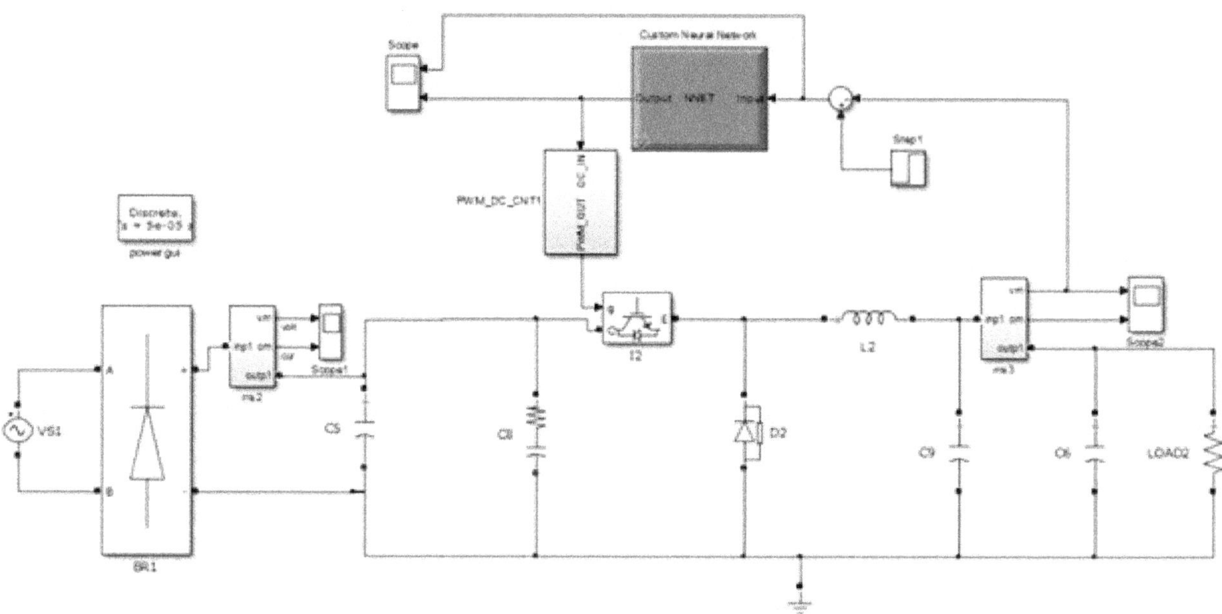

Fig.6 Neural Network Controller for DC-DC (Boost) Power Converter Circuit

- **How It Works:**
  - **Feedforward Neural Networks** are trained on historical data to map the relationship between inputs (e.g., voltage, current) and outputs (e.g., switching states, power levels).
  - **Recurrent Neural Networks (RNNs)** are useful for time-series predictions, allowing the system to predict future states based on past and present data, which is critical for managing fluctuating renewable energy inputs.
  - Once trained, these neural networks can generate control actions, such as determining the optimal switching sequence for a converter to maximize efficiency or minimize power loss.

- **Applications:**
  - **Real-Time Inverter Control**: Neural networks can adjust the switching patterns of inverters to achieve higher power quality and reduce harmonic distortion.
  - **Power Loss Minimization**: By continuously learning from the system's operation, neural networks can minimize energy losses during power conversion, especially under varying load and environmental conditions.

Reinforcement Learning for Control

Reinforcement Learning (RL) is a powerful method for developing autonomous control strategies. Unlike supervised learning, RL learns by interacting with the environment, receiving feedback in the form of rewards or penalties, and adjusting its behavior to maximize cumulative rewards over time.

- **How It Works:**
  - The RL agent (which controls the converter) interacts with the power system, making decisions on control actions (e.g., voltage regulation, switching states).
  - For each action, the agent receives feedback (e.g., power quality, system stability), which serves as a reward or penalty.
  - Over time, the agent learns the best control strategies through exploration and exploitation, continuously improving its performance as it interacts with more data.
- **Advantages:**
  - **Autonomous Learning:** RL algorithms can discover optimal control strategies without human intervention, making them ideal for systems where conditions are constantly changing (e.g., renewable energy integration).
  - **Dynamic Adaptation:** RL agents can adapt to new environments or operational conditions by continuously learning and updating their control policies.
- **Applications in Power Converters:**
  - **Grid-Tied Inverters:** RL algorithms can learn how to efficiently manage the power flow between renewable sources and the grid, optimizing voltage and frequency regulation.
  - **Battery Management Systems:** RL is used to optimize the charging and discharging cycles of batteries in conjunction with renewable energy sources, ensuring optimal performance and longevity of energy storage systems.

4.3 Real-Time Optimization and Control of Renewable Energy Systems

In renewable energy systems, the ability to perform real-time optimization and control is crucial for handling the variability and unpredictability of sources like solar and wind. Machine learning plays a pivotal role in achieving this by enabling systems to adapt and optimize performance in real-time.

What is Real-Time Optimization?

Real-time optimization refers to the process of continuously adjusting control parameters and operational settings to maximize the performance of a system in real-time. For renewable energy systems, this often means managing the dynamic interaction between power converters, energy storage, and the grid to ensure optimal energy conversion, minimal losses, and stability.

- **How It Works:**
  - **Data Collection:** Sensors and measurement devices monitor critical variables such as voltage, current, temperature, and power output.
  - **Machine Learning Models:** These models process the real-time data to predict future system states and calculate the optimal control actions.

- **Feedback Control Loop**: The system uses the machine learning model's predictions to adjust converter settings (such as switching frequency or duty cycle) on the fly, responding to changes in energy input (e.g., solar irradiance) and demand (e.g., load variations).

Key Technologies Enabling Real-Time Control:

1. **Model Predictive Control (MPC)**:
    - **Purpose**: MPC is a control strategy that predicts future behavior of the system based on current and past data, optimizing control actions over a time horizon.
    - **Application**: MPC is used in power converters to anticipate future changes in renewable energy input (such as fluctuating solar radiation) and adjust converter operations to maintain stable and efficient energy conversion.
2. **Neural Networks for Real-Time Control**:
    - **Purpose**: Neural networks can make rapid predictions based on real-time data, allowing converters to adjust switching patterns, voltage levels, and power flow dynamically.
    - **Application**: In solar inverters, for instance, neural networks can dynamically adjust MPPT (Maximum Power Point Tracking) algorithms in real-time to ensure maximum energy harvesting from solar panels.
3. **Reinforcement Learning for Autonomous Control**:
    - **Purpose**: Reinforcement learning can enable converters to autonomously learn optimal control policies by interacting with the environment, adjusting to varying input conditions such as fluctuating wind speeds or changing grid demands.
    - **Application**: RL is used for real-time power distribution in smart grids, where it learns how to balance energy flows from renewable sources, battery storage, and the grid to ensure efficiency and stability.

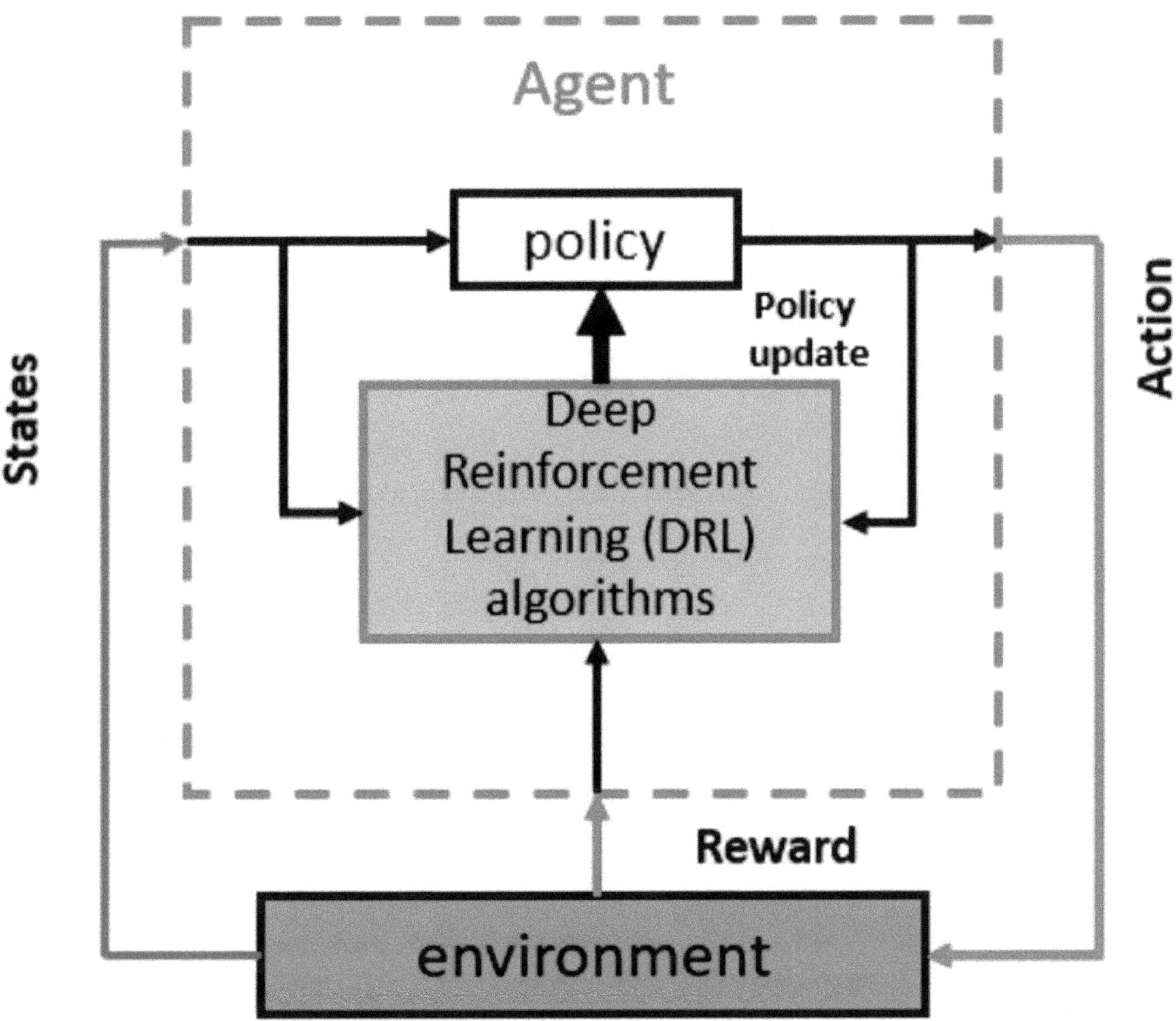

Fig 7. The general framework of Reinforcement Learning

Challenges in Real-Time Optimization:

- **Latency and Computational Power**: Real-time optimization requires fast processing of large amounts of data. Machine learning algorithms, especially deep learning and reinforcement learning models, need to be efficient enough to handle these tasks in milliseconds.
- **Integration with Legacy Systems**: Many renewable energy systems still use traditional control methods. Integrating machine learning-based control strategies with existing infrastructure requires careful consideration of compatibility and interoperability.

System Stability: Ensuring stability during real-time control is crucial. Machine learning models must be able to react appropriately to unforeseen changes without causing instability in the power system.

CHAPTER FIVE

Machine Learning for Predictive Maintenance in Power Electronics

Predictive maintenance leverages machine learning and data analytics to predict when power electronic components are likely to fail, allowing maintenance to be performed before actual failure occurs. This minimizes downtime, reduces maintenance costs, and enhances the reliability of renewable energy systems. Machine learning enables real-time monitoring, early failure detection, and anomaly detection, making it an essential tool for maintaining complex power electronics systems.

Condition Monitoring of Power Electronics Components

Condition monitoring involves continuously tracking the health and performance of power electronics components, such as inverters, rectifiers, and converters. This is done by collecting data on various operational parameters like temperature, voltage, current, and switching frequency.

How Machine Learning Improves Condition Monitoring

Machine learning can process large volumes of sensor data in real time, detecting subtle patterns and anomalies that may indicate the early stages of component degradation or failure. Unlike traditional threshold-based systems, machine learning models can identify issues based on complex, non-linear relationships in the data.

- **Data Sources**: Sensors attached to power electronics components generate real-time data, including thermal performance, electrical characteristics, and mechanical vibrations.
- **Feature Extraction**: Machine learning models can extract useful features from this raw data, such as temperature drift, voltage irregularities, or unusual current spikes, which may indicate a future issue.
- **Models Used**:
    - **Regression models**: Used to predict the degradation over time by analyzing historical data of components under similar operational conditions.
    - **Neural Networks**: These can model more complex relationships between operational parameters and component health.

Applications:

- **Inverter Monitoring in Solar Systems**: Condition monitoring ensures that the inverter, a critical part of the system, is operating efficiently and detects when its performance is degrading, potentially due to issues like capacitor aging or thermal stresses.
- **Power Converters in Wind Turbines**: Constant monitoring of converters, which handle fluctuating input power from wind turbines, can identify operational irregularities, such as overheating or overvoltage, long before they lead to system failures.

5.1 Failure Prediction and Diagnostics

Failure prediction focuses on forecasting when a power electronic component will fail, while diagnostics identifies the underlying cause of the failure. Machine learning enables accurate predictions and diagnostics by analyzing historical and real-time data.

How Machine Learning Enhances Failure Prediction

Machine learning algorithms can process vast datasets of operational data to recognize patterns associated with the normal degradation of components. By continuously learning from this data, models can predict the remaining useful life (RUL) of components or pinpoint when a failure is imminent.

- **Prognostics Algorithms:**
    - **Survival Analysis:** Predicts the probability of failure over time, helping determine when preventive action should be taken.
    - **Support Vector Machines (SVM):** These are used to classify data and predict failures based on past operational conditions.
    - **Recurrent Neural Networks (RNNs):** By considering the temporal nature of data, RNNs are effective at modeling time-series data to predict component failures over time.
- **Failure Diagnostics:** When a failure occurs, machine learning algorithms help determine the root cause by comparing the faulty data to past patterns of failures. This allows for rapid and accurate diagnosis, reducing system downtime.

Applications:

- **Capacitor Wear in Power Inverters:** Capacitors are among the most failure-prone components in power electronics. By tracking parameters like voltage ripple and temperature, machine learning models can predict when capacitors are likely to fail due to aging.
- **IGBT (Insulated-Gate Bipolar Transistor) Failure in Converters:** IGBTs are critical for switching operations in converters. Machine learning models analyze thermal stress and switching patterns to predict when an IGBT is nearing the end of its useful life, ensuring timely replacements.

5.2 Applications of Anomaly Detection in Renewable Energy Converters

Anomaly detection is a critical application of machine learning for identifying unusual patterns in system behavior that may indicate faults or malfunctions in renewable energy converters. These anomalies could be early warnings of system instability, component failure, or suboptimal performance.

How Machine Learning Aids Anomaly Detection

Machine learning models, especially unsupervised learning algorithms, can learn the normal operational patterns of power electronics components. Once trained, these models detect anomalies by flagging deviations from typical behavior.

- **Types of Anomalies:**
    - **Point Anomalies:** A single data point deviates significantly from the expected range (e.g., a sudden spike in voltage).

  - **Contextual Anomalies**: An observation is anomalous only in its specific context (e.g., high temperature during normal operation but within acceptable limits when under heavy load).
  - **Collective Anomalies**: A series of data points exhibit an unusual pattern, signaling a gradual performance degradation or a fault.

- **Techniques for Anomaly Detection**:

  - **Autoencoders**: Neural networks used for unsupervised anomaly detection, which learn a compressed representation of normal data. Any data point that cannot be effectively compressed (reconstructed) is flagged as an anomaly.
  - **K-Nearest Neighbors (KNN)**: Identifies anomalies by comparing each data point to its nearest neighbors. If a point is far from others, it is considered an anomaly.
  - **Isolation Forests**: A tree-based ensemble method that isolates anomalies by partitioning data points. Anomalies are isolated quickly, as they tend to lie in sparse regions of the data.

Applications:

- **Solar Power Converters**: Machine learning models can detect when converters are operating outside of normal efficiency ranges due to environmental factors like dust accumulation on solar panels or internal component wear.
- **Wind Turbine Power Electronics**: In wind turbines, sudden changes in converter performance, such as voltage fluctuations or irregular switching frequencies, can be identified early using anomaly detection, preventing catastrophic system failures.

CHAPTER SIX

Forecasting and Scheduling of Renewable Energy Using Machine Learning

Renewable energy sources, such as solar and wind, are highly variable and intermittent, making it challenging to integrate them efficiently into the grid. Machine learning has emerged as a powerful tool to address these challenges by improving the accuracy of energy production forecasting, demand response, and load forecasting, and optimizing the dispatch and scheduling of renewable energy. By leveraging historical data and real-time information, machine learning enhances the reliability, efficiency, and economic viability of renewable energy systems.

6.1 Energy Production Forecasting (Solar, Wind)

One of the primary challenges in integrating renewable energy into the grid is accurately predicting the power output from sources like solar and wind. These energy sources are dependent on weather conditions, which can fluctuate significantly. Machine learning models have proven to be highly effective in forecasting energy production by analyzing large datasets of historical weather patterns, real-time meteorological data, and other relevant factors.

A. **Solar Energy Forecasting**

Solar energy generation depends on factors such as sunlight intensity, cloud cover, temperature, and the angle of solar panels. Accurate forecasting requires the ability to predict these variables and how they will influence solar energy output.

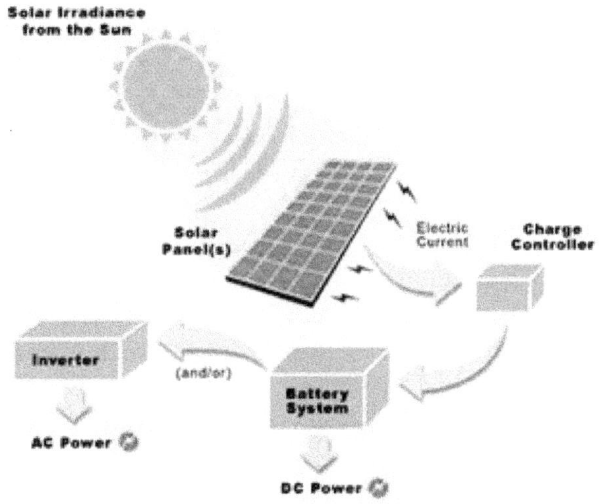

Fig 8. Solar renewable Energy Forecasting

- **How Machine Learning Enhances Solar Forecasting:**

  - **Supervised Learning Models:** Machine learning models, such as linear regression, support vector machines (SVM), and neural networks, are trained on historical solar radiation data and weather variables. These models learn patterns in how weather affects solar output, allowing for accurate predictions.
  - **Feature Engineering:** Important features, such as solar irradiance, temperature, and panel orientation, are extracted from weather data and used to train machine learning models.
  - **Hybrid Models:** Combining physical models of solar energy production with machine learning models can further improve the accuracy of forecasts by capturing both the deterministic and stochastic elements of solar power generation.

- **Applications:**

  - **Short-Term Forecasting:** Solar farms use machine learning models to predict energy output for the next few hours or days, helping grid operators balance supply and demand.
  - **Long-Term Forecasting:** Utilities rely on long-term forecasts to plan capacity expansions, maintenance, and energy trading strategies.

A. **Wind Energy Forecasting**

Wind energy production is highly variable, as it depends on wind speed, direction, air density, and other meteorological factors. Machine learning models are used to predict wind speeds at specific locations, enabling more accurate forecasts of wind power generation.

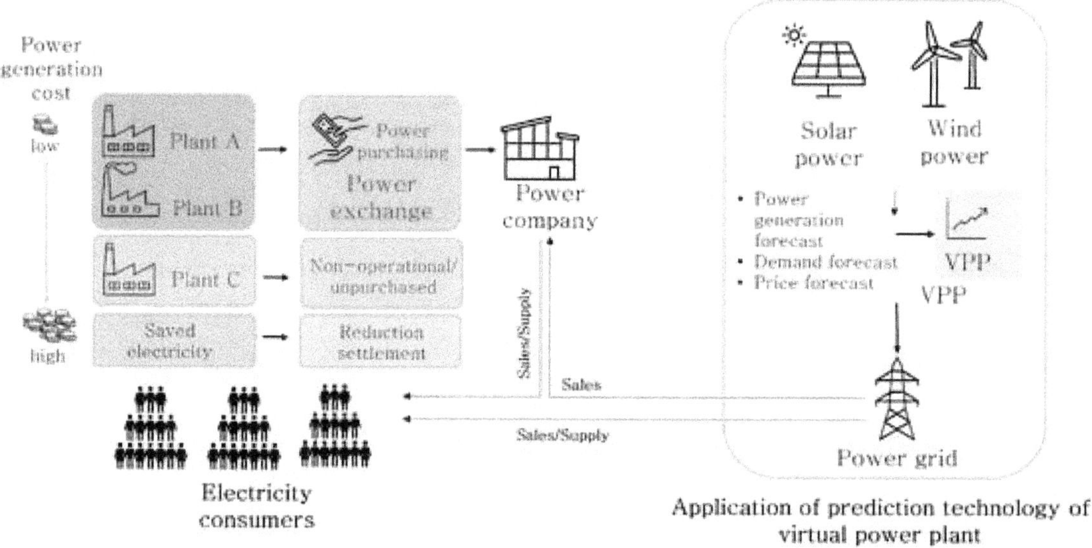

Fig .9 Wind Renewable Energy Forecasting

- **How Machine Learning Enhances Wind Forecasting:**

  - **Time-Series Forecasting:** Recurrent neural networks (RNNs) and long short-term memory (LSTM) networks are used to model the temporal dynamics of wind speed and direction, improving the accuracy of short- and medium-term forecasts.

  - **Geospatial Data Analysis:** Machine learning models incorporate data from multiple wind farms, satellite imagery, and meteorological stations to make regional wind power forecasts.
  - **Wind Turbine Efficiency Models:** Machine learning helps model the efficiency of wind turbines under varying wind conditions, improving energy yield predictions.

- **Applications:**

  - **Day-Ahead Forecasting:** Accurate wind forecasts for the next 24 hours are critical for grid stability, helping system operators plan for fluctuations in power generation.
  - **Intra-Day Forecasting:** Wind farm operators use machine learning to predict short-term variations in wind energy output, allowing for real-time adjustments to power dispatch strategies.

6.2 Demand Response and Load Forecasting

Accurately predicting energy demand (load forecasting) and coordinating demand response programs are crucial for maintaining the balance between supply and demand in renewable energy systems. Machine learning techniques, such as regression models, time-series analysis, and classification algorithms, play a vital role in load forecasting and optimizing demand response.

Load Forecasting

Load forecasting refers to predicting the amount of electrical energy that will be consumed by consumers over a specific period. Accurate load forecasting ensures that the grid is prepared to meet demand, even when integrating intermittent renewable sources like solar and wind.

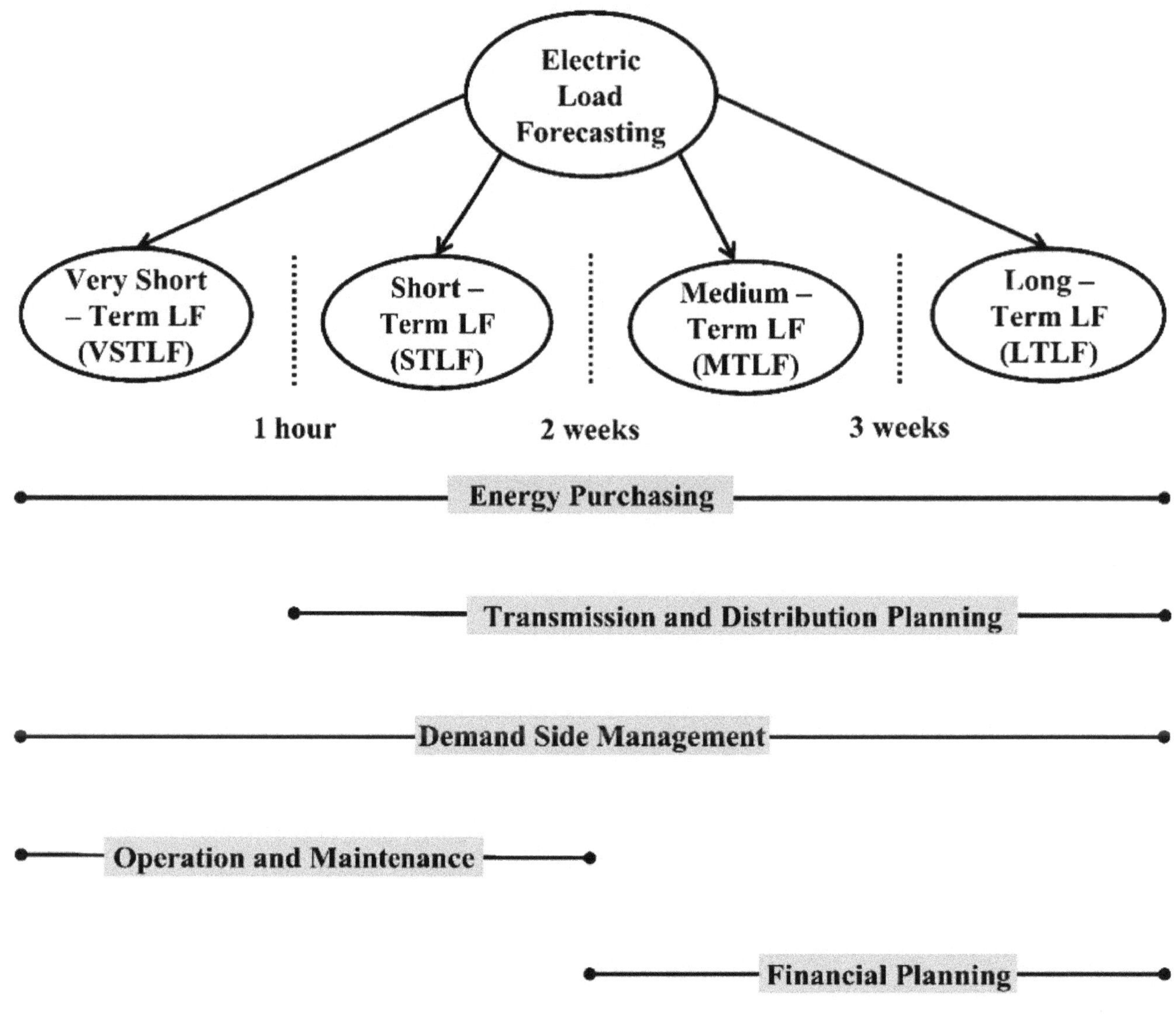

Fig.10 Load Forecasting

- **How Machine Learning Improves Load Forecasting:**
  - **Short-Term Load Forecasting:** Machine learning models are trained on historical consumption patterns and real-time data, such as temperature, time of day, and consumer behavior, to predict demand over the next few hours or days.
  - **Long-Term Load Forecasting:** For long-term forecasting, machine learning models analyze trends in population growth, economic development, and industrial activity to predict future energy consumption patterns.
  - **Techniques Used:** Linear regression, decision trees, neural networks, and ensemble methods are commonly used for load forecasting. Time-series models, such as ARIMA and LSTMs, capture the temporal dependencies in electricity demand.

- **Applications:**

- **Grid Stability**: Accurate load forecasts help grid operators plan energy production and storage strategies, ensuring stability and avoiding blackouts.
- **Energy Trading**: Utilities and energy traders use load forecasts to make informed decisions about purchasing and selling energy in wholesale markets.

Demand Response

Demand response refers to adjusting energy consumption in response to supply conditions. For example, consumers can be incentivized to reduce their usage during peak demand times or when renewable energy supply is low. Machine learning is used to predict consumer behavior, optimize pricing signals, and automate demand response actions.

- **How Machine Learning Enhances Demand Response**:
  - **Consumer Behaviour Prediction**: Machine learning models analyze historical consumption data and external factors (e.g., weather, events) to predict when consumers are likely to reduce or increase energy usage.
  - **Automated Demand Response**: Machine learning algorithms can automate demand response by adjusting thermostats, lighting, and industrial machinery in real-time, based on grid conditions and price signals.
  - **Dynamic Pricing Models**: Utilities use machine learning to forecast demand and dynamically adjust energy prices, encouraging consumers to shift their energy use to off-peak times.
- **Applications**:
  - **Residential Demand Response**: Smart meters and home energy management systems use machine learning to optimize energy usage, reducing costs for consumers and balancing grid demand.
  - **Industrial Demand Response**: Large industrial consumers participate in demand response programs by temporarily reducing their energy consumption during peak demand periods, based on real-time machine learning forecasts.

6.3 Optimizing Renewable Energy Dispatch and Scheduling

The dispatch and scheduling of renewable energy resources involve determining when and how much energy should be produced and delivered to meet demand. Machine learning plays a key role in optimizing these processes, ensuring that renewable energy is integrated efficiently into the grid while minimizing costs and maximizing system reliability.

Optimizing Energy Dispatch

Energy dispatch refers to the real-time allocation of energy resources to meet demand. Given the intermittent nature of renewable energy sources, machine learning models are used to predict supply and demand fluctuations and optimize the dispatch of renewable energy, storage, and conventional power plants.

- **How Machine Learning Enhances Energy Dispatch**:
  - **Predictive Algorithms**: Machine learning models predict renewable energy generation, demand patterns, and grid conditions, enabling optimal dispatch decisions.
  - **Real-Time Optimization**: Machine learning techniques, such as reinforcement learning and optimization algorithms, are used to continuously adjust dispatch strategies in real time, responding to changes in energy supply and demand.
  - **Hybrid Systems**: In hybrid systems that include both renewable energy and conventional power plants, machine learning models help determine when to prioritize renewable energy, when to use stored energy (e.g.,

batteries), and when to dispatch conventional power plants.

- **Applications**:
  - **Battery Energy Storage Systems (BESS)**: Machine learning is used to optimize the charging and discharging of batteries in response to renewable energy production and demand forecasts, maximizing efficiency and prolonging battery life.
  - **Grid-Tied Renewable Systems**: Machine learning models predict when to inject renewable energy into the grid based on supply and demand forecasts, ensuring grid stability and minimizing energy losses.

Scheduling of Renewable Energy

Scheduling refers to the advance planning of energy production and dispatch over a given time horizon. Machine learning helps optimize scheduling by analyzing weather forecasts, load predictions, and system constraints.

- **How Machine Learning Improves Scheduling**:
  - **Day-Ahead Scheduling**: Machine learning models are used to schedule renewable energy production for the next 24 hours based on weather forecasts and demand predictions. This helps system operators plan energy dispatch and storage strategies.
  - **Intra-Day Scheduling**: Machine learning models update energy schedules throughout the day, adjusting for real-time changes in weather and demand conditions.
  - **Economic Dispatch**: Machine learning optimizes the economic dispatch of renewable energy, balancing cost, efficiency, and grid reliability.

- **Applications**:
  - **Solar and Wind Farms**: Machine learning optimizes the operation and scheduling of renewable energy farms, ensuring that energy is dispatched at the right time to meet demand while minimizing costs.
  - **Microgrids**: In microgrids, machine learning models balance the scheduling of renewable energy, storage, and backup generation to ensure reliability and cost-effectiveness.

CHAPTER SEVEN

Fault Detection and Diagnosis in Renewable Energy Systems

Fault detection and diagnosis (FDD) are critical aspects of maintaining the operational efficiency and reliability of renewable energy systems. As solar, wind, and hybrid energy systems become more prevalent, the complexity of monitoring and identifying faults increases. Machine learning techniques are now used to enhance the accuracy and speed of fault detection, allowing systems to continue running efficiently while minimizing downtime and repair costs. In this chapter, we explore how machine learning aids in fault detection, the diagnostic methods for key renewable energy components, and real-world case studies.

7.1 Machine Learning Techniques for Fault Detection

Fault detection involves identifying abnormalities in the performance of renewable energy systems before they cause serious damage or lead to failures. Machine learning techniques enable automated and highly accurate detection of these faults by analyzing vast amounts of operational data in real-time.

Types of Machine Learning Models Used for Fault Detection:

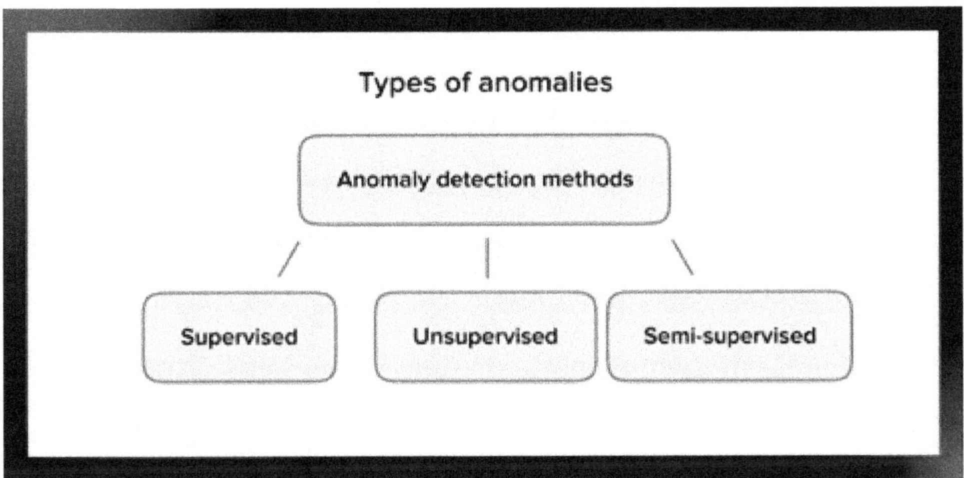

Fig11.Types of anomalies

1. **Supervised Learning**: In supervised learning, historical data labeled with "normal" and "faulty" conditions is used to train machine learning models. Once trained, these models can classify incoming data to identify whether the system is operating correctly or if a fault has occurred.

    - **Techniques**: Decision Trees, Support Vector Machines (SVM), K-Nearest Neighbors (KNN)

2. **Unsupervised Learning**: These models are useful when there is limited labeled data. Unsupervised techniques learn the normal operating behavior of a system and detect deviations from this behavior, which may indicate faults.
   - **Techniques**: Clustering (K-means), Autoencoders, Isolation Forests
3. **Reinforcement Learning**: This is used in fault detection for real-time adaptive control of renewable energy systems. The algorithm continuously learns from the environment, adjusting its decisions to detect and respond to faults dynamically.
   - **Techniques**: Q-learning, Deep Q-networks
4. **Anomaly Detection Models**: These models detect outliers or unusual patterns in data, which could be early signs of faults.
   - **Techniques**: Principal Component Analysis (PCA), One-Class SVM, Neural Networks

Benefits of Machine Learning for Fault Detection:

- **Real-Time Monitoring**: Machine learning models analyze real-time data streams, allowing immediate detection of faults.
- **High Sensitivity**: These models can detect even minor deviations in system performance, preventing larger failures.
- **Scalability**: Machine learning models can scale across different renewable energy systems, from small-scale solar installations to large wind farms.

7.2 Diagnostic Methods for Solar Inverters, Wind Turbines, and Hybrid Systems

After fault detection, diagnosing the root cause is essential for timely repairs and minimizing operational downtime. Each renewable energy technology has unique components and failure modes, requiring tailored diagnostic methods.

Solar Inverter Diagnostics:

Solar inverters, which convert DC power from solar panels to AC power for grid integration, are prone to various faults, such as grid fluctuations, component wear, or temperature overload. Machine learning models improve diagnostic capabilities by analyzing data from the inverter's sensors and identifying patterns that indicate specific failure modes.

- **Common Inverter Faults:**
  - **DC-Link Capacitor Failure**: This component can degrade over time, leading to power conversion inefficiencies. Machine learning models monitor voltage and current levels to detect anomalies indicating capacitor wear.
  - **Overheating**: Excessive heat can cause inverter breakdown. Temperature sensors provide data for predictive models that alert operators before the inverter reaches critical temperature levels.
- **Diagnostic Approaches:**

- **Classification Models**: Support Vector Machines (SVM) or neural networks are trained to classify different types of inverter faults based on operational data.
- **Thermal Analysis**: Data-driven models can predict overheating in inverter circuits based on temperature readings and environmental conditions.

Wind Turbine Diagnostics:

Wind turbines operate under harsh conditions, making them susceptible to a wide range of faults, such as gearbox failures, blade damage, or generator malfunctions. Machine learning models use sensor data from vibration monitors, strain gauges, and other sources to diagnose issues and prevent breakdowns.

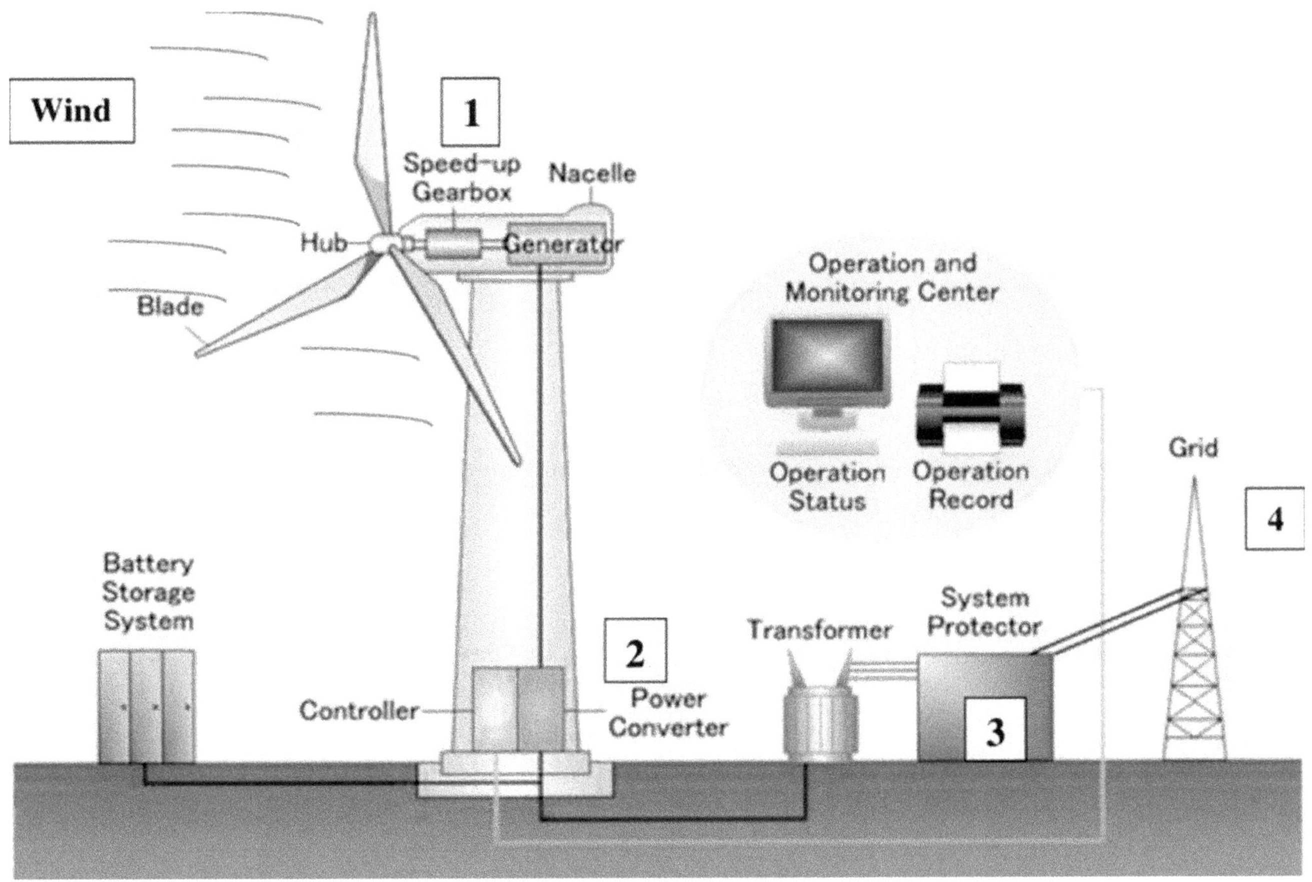

Fig .12 diagnostic process for wind turbines using machine learning.

- **Common Wind Turbine Faults**:
  - **Gearbox Faults**: Gearboxes are a critical component in wind turbines, and mechanical wear or misalignment can lead to failure. Vibration data is analyzed by machine learning models to detect early signs of wear.
  - **Blade Damage**: Wind turbine blades can suffer from fatigue or damage due to high winds or debris. Machine learning models trained on acoustic and vibration data can detect subtle signs of blade degradation.
- **Diagnostic Approaches**:
  - **Vibration Analysis**: Machine learning models process vibration data to detect misalignments or mechanical wear in the gearbox.

  - **Acoustic Monitoring:** Sound sensors on the blades or nacelle detect unusual noise patterns. Models such as autoencoders can detect changes in these acoustic signals, helping diagnose blade damage.

Hybrid Systems Diagnostics:

Hybrid renewable energy systems that combine solar, wind, and battery storage face additional challenges in fault diagnosis due to the complexity of managing multiple energy sources and their interactions. Machine learning offers a solution by integrating data from various components into a single diagnostic framework.

- **Common Hybrid System Faults:**
  - **Battery Failures:** Energy storage systems in hybrid setups are prone to thermal runaway or capacity degradation. Machine learning models predict battery failures by analyzing charge/discharge cycles, temperature, and voltage patterns.
  - **Grid Integration Issues:** Hybrid systems connected to the grid may experience synchronization faults or power quality issues. Real-time data from both generation and storage systems allows machine learning models to detect and resolve these integration problems.
- **Diagnostic Approaches:**
  - **Integrated Diagnostic Models:** Machine learning models analyze data from solar panels, wind turbines, and batteries in parallel, providing a holistic view of system health.
  - **Predictive Maintenance Algorithms:** Using machine learning for predictive maintenance, hybrid systems can schedule repairs or replacements before a fault leads to a total system failure.

7.3 Case Studies in Fault Detection

To illustrate the effectiveness of machine learning in fault detection, several real-world case studies can be presented. These case studies highlight how machine learning models have successfully identified and diagnosed faults in renewable energy systems, reducing downtime and improving operational efficiency.

Case Study 1: Fault Detection in a Solar PV Farm Using Machine Learning

In a large solar photovoltaic (PV) farm, machine learning models were implemented to monitor the performance of solar inverters and detect faults early. By analyzing data from inverters, such as output voltage, current, and temperature, machine learning models were able to detect issues such as DC-link capacitor degradation and partial shading on panels. Early fault detection reduced system downtime by 20% and improved overall energy output.

- **Key Insights:**
  - SVM models were used to classify inverter faults with 95% accuracy.
  - Anomaly detection methods identified shading issues within hours of occurrence, enabling prompt maintenance.

Case Study 2: Predictive Maintenance of Wind Turbines with Machine Learning

A wind farm deployed machine learning models to predict gearbox failures in wind turbines. By analyzing real-time vibration data from sensors installed in the turbine gearbox, the models detected early signs of wear, allowing for repairs to be scheduled during low-demand periods. This reduced maintenance costs and prevented unscheduled downtime.

- **Key Insights**:
  - Vibration analysis models predicted gearbox failures three weeks in advance, providing ample time for repairs.
  - Maintenance costs were reduced by 15%, and turbine availability increased by 5%.

Case Study 3: Hybrid Energy System Fault Detection in Microgrids

In a microgrid combining solar, wind, and battery storage, machine learning was used to detect faults in the energy storage system. By monitoring charge and discharge patterns, as well as temperature data from the battery, the models predicted thermal runaway incidents before they occurred, preventing significant damage to the system.

- **Key Insights**:
  - Neural network models accurately predicted battery overheating, reducing the likelihood of system failure by 30%.
  - The hybrid system maintained uninterrupted operation, even during peak energy demand periods.

CHAPTER EIGHT

Optimization of Renewable Energy Integration with Machine Learning

As renewable energy sources like solar, wind, and hybrid systems become integral parts of modern energy grids, optimizing their integration is essential for ensuring efficiency, reliability, and sustainability. Machine learning (ML) plays a crucial role in enhancing the management of energy storage, optimizing power flow in microgrids, and integrating battery and hybrid systems. By using ML algorithms, energy producers can better manage fluctuations in renewable energy production, improve storage utilization, and optimize overall energy dispatch.

8.1 Energy Storage Management

Energy storage systems (ESS) are key components in renewable energy systems, as they balance the intermittent nature of renewable sources. Batteries, pumped hydro storage, and other energy storage technologies store excess energy during times of low demand and release it when demand exceeds production. Machine learning can significantly improve the management of energy storage, enhancing efficiency and prolonging battery life.

Challenges in Energy Storage Management:

- **Intermittency of Renewable Sources**: Solar and wind energy generation can fluctuate due to weather conditions, leading to inconsistent energy supply. Effective storage management ensures that energy is available when needed.
- **Battery Degradation**: Batteries degrade over time due to repeated charge and discharge cycles. Proper management strategies are required to minimize degradation and extend battery life.
- **Cost-Effectiveness**: Maximizing the efficiency of energy storage systems helps reduce operational costs by optimizing charging and discharging schedules.

Machine Learning Solutions for Storage Management:

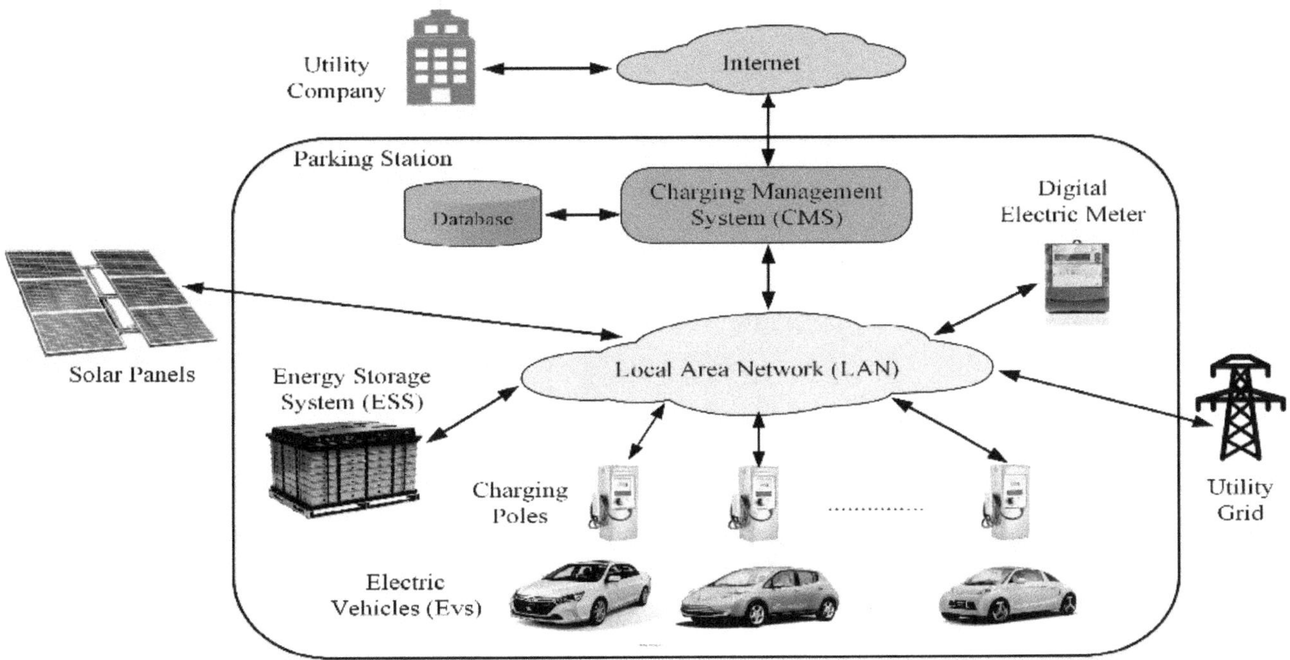

Fig.13 EV charging and discharging in a parking station with ESS, PVS, and the power grid

1. **Battery State-of-Charge (SoC) and State-of-Health (SoH) Prediction**: Machine learning models are used to predict the SoC and SoH of batteries in real-time. By accurately estimating the battery's available charge and its health status, ML models optimize when to charge or discharge energy, prolonging battery life.

    ◦ **Techniques**: Recurrent Neural Networks (RNNs), Long Short-Term Memory (LSTM) models, and decision trees analyze historical usage data, environmental conditions, and charge/discharge patterns.

2. **Optimal Charging and Discharging Strategies**: Machine learning algorithms can predict periods of peak demand and excess energy generation, allowing for optimized charging and discharging strategies that reduce wear and maximize energy efficiency.

    ◦ **Techniques**: Reinforcement learning models continuously adapt charging/discharging strategies in real-time based on predicted energy demand and generation, improving efficiency.

3. **Energy Storage Allocation**: For hybrid systems with multiple energy storage units (e.g., batteries, supercapacitors), machine learning models determine the most efficient use of each storage type, optimizing energy dispatch and system efficiency.

    Applications:

- **Residential and Industrial Storage Systems**: ML-based storage management systems are increasingly used in residential solar systems, commercial buildings, and industrial plants to ensure optimal energy use and minimize costs.
- **Grid-Scale Battery Management**: Utility companies use ML algorithms to manage large-scale battery storage systems, optimizing energy dispatch during peak hours and improving grid stability.

8.2 Power Flow Optimization in Microgrids

Microgrids, which are localized grids that can operate independently or in conjunction with the main grid, play a pivotal role in integrating renewable energy into power systems. By incorporating distributed energy resources (DERs), such as solar panels, wind turbines, and energy storage, microgrids can efficiently manage energy generation and consumption at a local level. Machine learning enhances power flow optimization within these microgrids, ensuring a reliable and balanced energy supply.

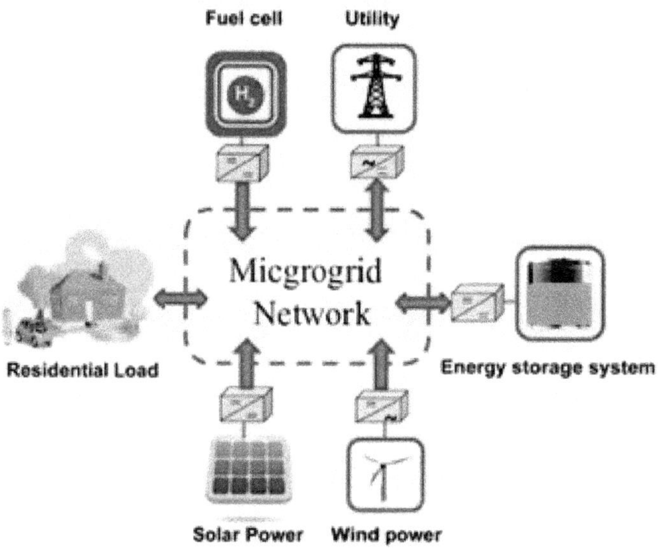

Fig.14 Microgrid Network

Challenges in Power Flow Optimization:

- **Intermittency of Renewables**: Microgrids heavily rely on renewable energy, which can lead to power imbalances if not managed properly.
- **Decentralized Control**: Unlike traditional grids, microgrids feature decentralized control mechanisms, which require advanced optimization strategies for energy flow.
- **Dynamic Load Management**: Microgrids must dynamically balance energy production and consumption, requiring real-time decision-making.

Machine Learning Solutions for Power Flow Optimization:

1. **Predictive Power Flow Models**: ML algorithms are used to forecast energy demand, renewable energy generation, and grid conditions. These forecasts enable microgrids to manage power flow proactively, ensuring that supply meets demand.

    - **Techniques**: Neural networks and time-series forecasting models (e.g., LSTMs) predict fluctuations in energy production and consumption patterns, enabling microgrids to adjust power flow accordingly.

2. **Decentralized Control Using Reinforcement Learning**: In microgrids with distributed energy resources (DERs), reinforcement learning algorithms are deployed to optimize power flow in real-time. These algorithms learn the optimal power dispatch strategy by interacting with the microgrid environment and adjusting energy flows to

minimize costs and maximize efficiency.

- **Techniques**: Multi-agent reinforcement learning models allow each DER to make independent decisions while coordinating with other resources in the microgrid.

3. **Load Balancing and Demand Response**: Machine learning models optimize load balancing by dynamically adjusting energy distribution between DERs and storage systems, ensuring that excess energy is stored or distributed when demand is high.

   - **Techniques**: Clustering algorithms group similar energy demand patterns, and ML-based predictive models forecast peak loads, allowing for preemptive load balancing and efficient demand response strategies.

Applications:

- **Islanded Microgrids**: Microgrids that are disconnected from the main grid, such as those in remote areas, rely on ML-based power flow optimization to manage limited energy resources efficiently.
- **Urban Microgrids**: In urban environments, microgrids use machine learning to optimize power flows between renewable sources, energy storage, and the main grid, ensuring a reliable and cost-effective energy supply.

8.3 Integration of Battery and Hybrid Energy Systems Using ML

Hybrid energy systems combine multiple renewable energy sources, such as solar, wind, and energy storage, to provide a more reliable and flexible power supply. Managing the integration of these diverse energy sources and optimizing their performance requires sophisticated control strategies. Machine learning has become a key enabler in managing hybrid systems, providing tools to optimize energy production, storage, and dispatch in real-time.

Challenges in Integrating Hybrid Energy Systems:

- **Synchronization of Different Energy Sources**: Coordinating the output of different energy sources, such as solar panels and wind turbines, while managing energy storage, requires precise timing and control to ensure efficient energy use.
- **Dynamic Energy Dispatch**: Hybrid systems must dynamically allocate energy based on real-time demand, renewable energy generation, and storage conditions.
- **Minimizing Curtailment**: Hybrid systems can experience energy curtailment (wasting excess energy) if production exceeds demand or storage capacity. Optimizing integration ensures minimal energy wastage.

Machine Learning Solutions for Hybrid Energy System Integration:

1. **Energy Production and Storage Coordination**: Machine learning models predict the output of solar, wind, and other renewable energy sources, coordinating this output with storage management strategies to ensure continuous power supply.

   - **Techniques**: Support Vector Machines (SVMs), neural networks, and decision trees analyze weather data, historical generation patterns, and load profiles to optimize energy dispatch from multiple sources.

2. **Real-Time Energy Dispatch Optimization**: In hybrid systems, machine learning algorithms optimize energy dispatch in real-time by analyzing current energy demand, production rates, and storage availability. These models continuously adjust energy allocation between different sources and storage systems to minimize costs and improve efficiency.

    ◦ **Techniques**: Reinforcement learning algorithms are used to adapt dispatch strategies dynamically, improving system efficiency under varying conditions.

3. **Hybrid System Stability and Reliability**: ML models monitor and control hybrid systems, ensuring stability by detecting potential faults and anomalies in energy production or storage. Predictive maintenance models reduce system downtime and improve overall reliability.

    ◦ **Techniques**: Anomaly detection algorithms, such as isolation forests and autoencoders, detect irregularities in system performance, preventing unexpected failures and maintaining system stability.

Applications:

- **Grid-Connected Hybrid Systems**: Machine learning optimizes the integration of hybrid systems with the main grid, managing energy dispatch to minimize reliance on conventional power sources.
- **Off-Grid Hybrid Systems:** In remote or isolated areas, ML-based hybrid systems ensure continuous power supply by efficiently managing local energy resources and storage.

CHAPTER NINE

Power Quality Improvement in Renewable Systems Using Machine Learning

Power quality in renewable energy systems is critical for ensuring stable, reliable, and efficient electricity supply. The integration of renewable energy sources such as solar and wind into the power grid introduces new challenges, particularly in terms of harmonics, reactive power, voltage stability, and frequency fluctuations. Machine learning (ML) offers advanced techniques for improving power quality, enabling adaptive control, filtering, and system stability in both grid-tied and islanded modes. This chapter explores how ML can address common power quality issues and enhance system performance.

9.1 Mitigating Harmonics and Reactive Power Issues

Renewable energy systems, particularly those that use power electronic devices such as inverters and converters, can introduce harmonic distortions and reactive power imbalances into the grid. These issues can degrade power quality, reduce the efficiency of the power system, and cause damage to sensitive equipment. Mitigating these issues is essential for maintaining the integrity of both local microgrids and larger grid systems.

Harmonics:

- **What Are Harmonics?** Harmonics are voltage or current waveforms that deviate from the fundamental frequency (typically 50 or 60 Hz) in a power system. They are often caused by non-linear loads and power electronic devices in renewable energy systems.
- **Impact on Power Systems**: Harmonic distortions can lead to increased heat in electrical equipment, malfunctioning of sensitive devices, and reduced system efficiency.

Reactive Power:

- **What Is Reactive Power?** Reactive power is the component of electricity that does not perform any useful work but is necessary for maintaining voltage levels in AC systems. However, imbalances in reactive power can cause voltage instability and increase transmission losses.
- **Impact on Power Systems:** If not managed properly, excess reactive power can lead to voltage sags, swells, and fluctuations in the grid, which compromises power quality.

Machine Learning Solutions for Mitigating Harmonics and Reactive Power:

1. **Harmonic Prediction and Mitigation**: ML algorithms can be used to predict and mitigate harmonic distortions by analyzing real-time power signals. These algorithms detect the presence of harmonic components and help design optimal filter settings to minimize distortions.

- **Techniques**: Neural networks and Support Vector Machines (SVMs) are trained to recognize harmonic patterns in power signals and suggest adaptive filtering techniques.

2. **Reactive Power Compensation**: Machine learning models analyze reactive power data and optimize the operation of compensating devices like capacitor banks or power factor correction units to balance reactive power in the system.

   - **Techniques**: Reinforcement learning algorithms can dynamically adjust reactive power compensators to maintain voltage stability while minimizing transmission losses.

3. **Voltage and Frequency Regulation**: By predicting voltage and frequency deviations caused by reactive power imbalances, ML models enable better control of inverters and voltage regulators to stabilize the grid.

   - **Techniques**: Regression models and neural networks are used to forecast voltage fluctuations and optimize inverter settings for voltage and frequency regulation.

Applications:

- **Grid-Tied Renewable Systems**: In grid-tied solar or wind farms, ML models are used to mitigate harmonic distortions and reactive power issues that arise due to grid interactions and inverter operations.
- **Industrial Power Systems**: In industrial setups, where large renewable systems are integrated, ML-based reactive power compensation improves voltage stability and reduces equipment wear.

9.2 Adaptive Filtering and Control Strategies

Traditional filtering and control strategies in renewable energy systems often rely on fixed settings that may not respond well to dynamic changes in power quality. Machine learning offers adaptive approaches that adjust filtering and control strategies in real-time based on system conditions. These adaptive solutions are critical for maintaining optimal power quality in both grid-tied and isolated renewable systems.

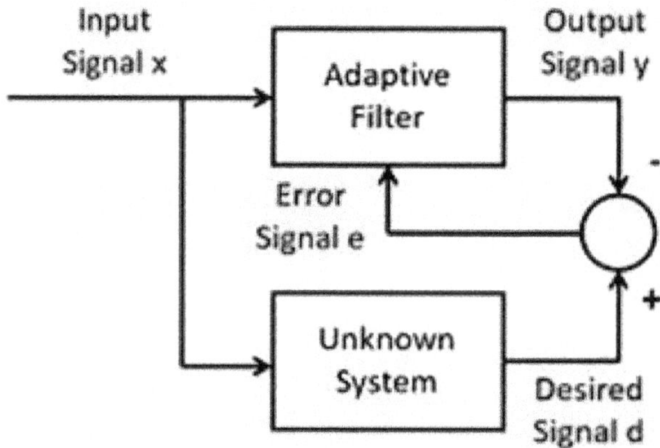

Fig.15 Adaptive Filter

Challenges in Traditional Filtering:

- **Fixed Filter Designs**: Traditional filters (such as passive or active filters) are designed for specific operating conditions and may not perform well under changing loads or power fluctuations, especially in renewable systems.
- **Dynamic Grid Conditions**: Power quality issues like harmonics and voltage sags can vary throughout the day based on changes in energy generation, consumption, and grid conditions.

Machine Learning Solutions for Adaptive Filtering:

1. **Adaptive Harmonic Filtering**: ML-based adaptive filters continuously monitor power quality metrics and adjust filter parameters to remove harmonic distortions as they arise.

    - **Techniques**: Reinforcement learning models adapt the filter parameters in real-time based on power signal feedback, ensuring that harmonics are kept within acceptable levels.

2. **Predictive Control Strategies**: Machine learning models predict power quality issues such as harmonics or voltage fluctuations based on historical and real-time data, allowing preemptive adjustments in control settings to improve power quality.

    - **Techniques**: Time-series forecasting models like Long Short-Term Memory (LSTM) networks analyze historical power quality data to predict future disturbances, enabling proactive adjustments.

3. **Intelligent Inverter Control**: Inverters, which convert DC power from renewable sources to AC, can introduce harmonics into the system. ML algorithms optimize inverter control settings to minimize these distortions and ensure smooth integration with the grid.

    - **Techniques**: Fuzzy logic controllers integrated with ML models dynamically adjust the inverter's operation based on the predicted power quality issues.

Applications:

- **Residential Solar Systems**: ML-based adaptive filters help homeowners maintain stable power quality even as solar generation fluctuates throughout the day.
- **Utility-Scale Wind Farms**: Wind turbines often introduce harmonics into the grid, especially during high wind conditions. Adaptive filtering strategies using ML ensure consistent power quality in these large installations.

9.3 Applications in Grid-Tied and Islanded Modes

Power quality management in renewable systems can vary significantly depending on whether the system is grid-tied or operating in islanded mode. In grid-tied systems, maintaining power quality is essential for smooth interaction with the main grid, while in islanded systems, maintaining voltage and frequency stability is paramount for local energy supply. Machine learning techniques offer tailored solutions for both scenarios.

Grid-Tied Mode:

- **Challenges**: In grid-tied renewable systems, power quality issues can arise from fluctuations in renewable energy generation and interactions with the larger grid. These systems must ensure harmonics are minimized, voltage levels are maintained, and reactive power is balanced.
- **ML Solutions**:

1. **Grid Synchronization**: Machine learning models analyze grid conditions and adjust inverter outputs to ensure smooth synchronization with the main grid, reducing power quality disturbances.
2. **Real-Time Power Factor Correction**: By using ML algorithms to monitor reactive power levels, grid-tied systems can dynamically adjust their power factor, improving energy efficiency and reducing losses.

Islanded Mode:

- **Challenges**: In islanded microgrids, renewable systems must independently manage voltage and frequency stability, as they are disconnected from the main grid. Power quality issues such as voltage sags or frequency variations must be corrected locally.
- **ML Solutions**:

1. **Frequency Regulation**: Machine learning models predict frequency variations caused by fluctuating renewable energy production, allowing islanded systems to adjust generator output or energy storage dispatch to maintain frequency stability.
2. **Voltage Control**: ML algorithms help islanded systems maintain stable voltage levels by adjusting the operation of local generation units and storage systems.

Applications:

- **Islanded Microgrids**: In rural or remote areas, ML models ensure consistent power quality by managing the local renewable generation and storage systems effectively.
- **Grid-Tied Commercial Solar**: Large commercial solar installations rely on ML-based solutions to ensure they meet grid power quality standards, allowing them to sell surplus energy without penalties.

CHAPTER TEN

Hybrid Machine Learning Models for Power Electronics

As the field of power electronics evolves, the integration of machine learning (ML) with traditional control methods offers significant potential for enhancing the performance, reliability, and efficiency of power electronic systems. Hybrid machine learning models combine the strengths of classical control techniques with the adaptive capabilities of ML, providing a robust framework for addressing complex challenges in power electronics. This chapter explores the integration of these methodologies, the use of ensemble models, and presents case studies of successful hybrid systems.

10.1 Combining Traditional Control Methods with Machine Learning

Traditional control methods, such as PID controllers, have long been the backbone of power electronics, providing reliable and stable operation. However, these methods often struggle with non-linearities, dynamic changes in system behavior, and uncertainties typical in renewable energy applications. By combining traditional control approaches with machine learning techniques, engineers can create hybrid models that leverage the best of both worlds.

Benefits of Hybrid Control Approaches:

1. **Adaptive Control**: Machine learning algorithms can analyze real-time data to adapt control strategies based on changing conditions, enhancing the responsiveness of traditional controllers.
2. **Improved Performance**: Hybrid models can outperform traditional control methods by learning from historical data and making informed decisions that optimize system performance.
3. **Robustness to Disturbances**: Integrating ML helps traditional control methods to better handle disturbances and uncertainties, improving system reliability.

Examples of Hybrid Control Approaches:

- **PID Controllers Enhanced with ML**: Machine learning can be employed to tune PID parameters dynamically based on real-time system responses. This results in optimized performance under varying operating conditions.

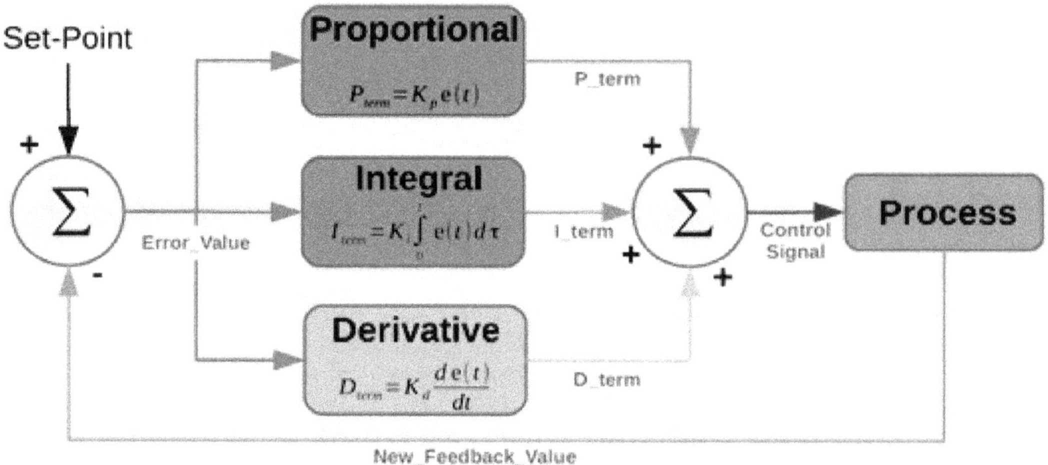

Fig.16 Block diagram of PID controller

- ◦ **Technique:** Reinforcement learning can be utilized to adapt PID settings to minimize tracking error and improve stability.

- **Model Predictive Control (MPC) with ML:** MPC can benefit from machine learning predictions about future system behavior, allowing for better decision-making regarding control actions over a defined time horizon.

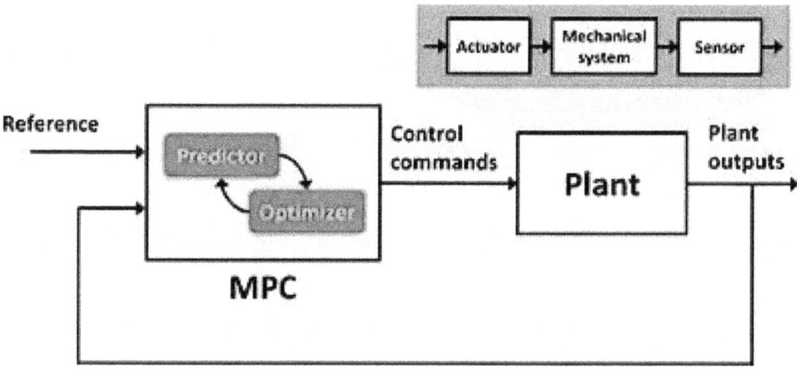

Fig.17 Model Predictive Control (MPC) with ML

- ◦ **Technique:** ML models predict future load demands or renewable generation patterns, enabling the MPC to optimize control actions accordingly.

10.2 Ensemble Models for Enhanced Reliability and Performance

Ensemble learning techniques combine multiple machine learning models to improve prediction accuracy and system performance. By leveraging the strengths of various algorithms, ensemble models can enhance the reliability and robustness of power electronic systems.

Key Benefits of Ensemble Models:

1. **Increased Accuracy**: By aggregating predictions from multiple models, ensemble methods reduce the likelihood of errors, providing more accurate control and prediction outcomes.
2. **Improved Generalization**: Ensemble models are less prone to overfitting compared to single models, making them better suited for complex and noisy data typical in power electronics applications.
3. **Robustness**: The combination of different algorithms ensures that if one model fails or performs poorly, others can compensate, enhancing the overall system reliability.

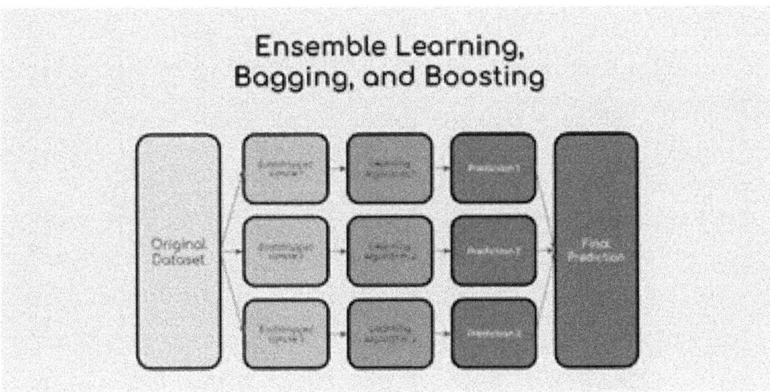

Fig.18 Ensemble learning Model Bagging and Boosting

Common Ensemble Techniques:

- **Bagging (Bootstrap Aggregating)**: This technique builds multiple versions of a model on different subsets of the training data and averages their predictions. Bagging is effective in reducing variance and improving model stability.
    - **Example**: Random Forests combine multiple decision trees to make more robust predictions about power system performance.
- **Boosting**: Boosting techniques sequentially apply models to focus on the errors made by previous models, effectively improving accuracy by giving more weight to difficult-to-predict instances.
    - **Example**: AdaBoost or Gradient Boosting can enhance predictive maintenance models by iteratively correcting mistakes in previous predictions.
- **Stacking**: Stacking combines different types of models, allowing a higher-level model to learn how to optimally combine their predictions.
    - **Example**: A stacking ensemble might use various regression models to predict energy production, with a meta-model refining the overall prediction.

10.3 Case Studies of Hybrid Systems

Real-world applications of hybrid machine learning models in power electronics demonstrate their potential to solve complex challenges in energy management, control, and optimization. This section highlights successful case studies where hybrid models have significantly improved system performance.

Case Study 1: Hybrid Control of Solar Inverters

A solar inverter system integrated a traditional PID controller with a machine learning model to optimize its operation in varying environmental conditions. The ML model was trained on historical data to predict optimal operating points based on temperature, irradiance, and load conditions. This hybrid approach resulted in improved efficiency and reduced energy losses compared to traditional control methods alone.

Case Study 2: Smart Grid Demand Response

In a smart grid application, a hybrid ensemble model combined multiple machine learning techniques to predict energy demand and optimize demand response strategies. By analyzing historical consumption data and incorporating real-time feedback, the ensemble model significantly improved demand forecasting accuracy, allowing for more effective energy management and resource allocation in the grid.

Case Study 3: Predictive Maintenance for Wind Turbines

Hybrid machine learning models have been employed in predictive maintenance for wind turbines, combining traditional fault detection methods with machine learning techniques to analyze sensor data. The models predict potential failures by learning from past operational data, enabling proactive maintenance and reducing downtime. This integration has led to enhanced reliability and efficiency in wind energy generation.

CHAPTER ELEVEN

AI-Driven Energy Management Systems

As the world increasingly shifts towards sustainable energy solutions, the need for efficient and intelligent energy management systems becomes paramount. AI-driven energy management systems utilize advanced algorithms and data analytics to optimize the generation, distribution, and consumption of energy. This chapter explores the design of these systems, the role of AI in managing a mix of renewable and conventional energy sources, and presents case studies highlighting successful smart grid integration.

11.1 Design of Smart Energy Management Systems

Smart energy management systems (EMS) integrate advanced technologies, data analytics, and artificial intelligence to optimize energy usage and improve operational efficiency. The design of such systems involves several key components and considerations:

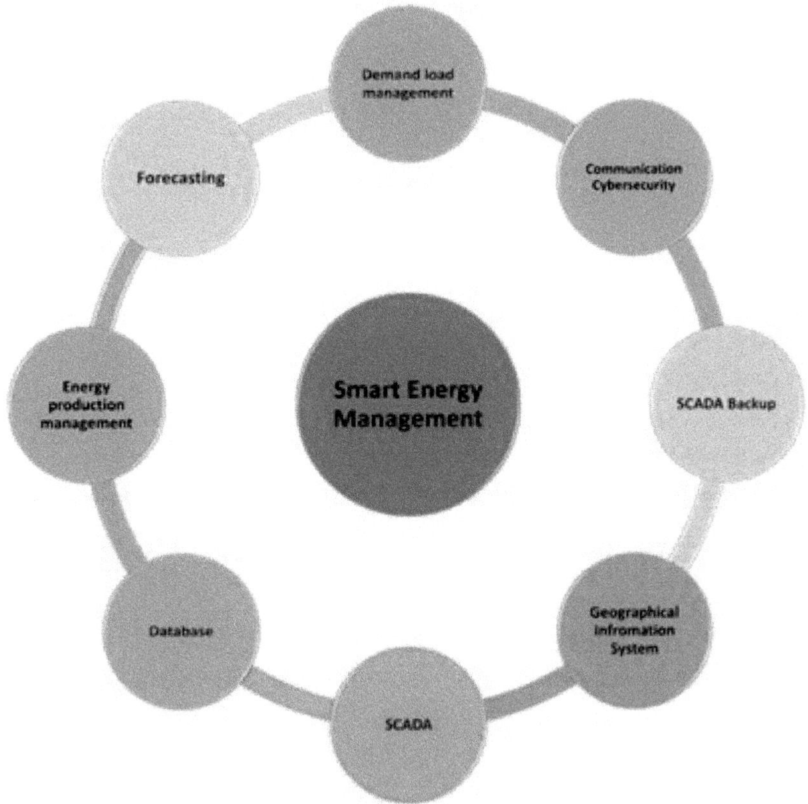

Fig.19 Smart Energy Management Systems

Key Components of Smart EMS:

1. **Data Acquisition**: Smart EMS collect data from various sources, including smart meters, sensors, and IoT devices, to monitor energy consumption and generation in real time.
   - **Importance**: Accurate data is crucial for making informed decisions about energy management and identifying potential areas for improvement.
2. **Data Analytics and Machine Learning**: The collected data is analyzed using machine learning algorithms to identify patterns, trends, and anomalies in energy usage.
   - **Techniques**: Regression analysis, clustering, and time-series forecasting can be applied to predict future energy demands and optimize resource allocation.
3. **Control and Optimization Algorithms**: AI-driven algorithms control the operation of energy systems, optimizing the generation and distribution of energy based on real-time data.
   - **Techniques**: Model Predictive Control (MPC) and reinforcement learning can be used to dynamically adjust energy flows and maximize efficiency.
4. **User Interfaces**: Intuitive dashboards and visualizations provide users with insights into energy usage patterns, cost savings, and performance metrics, enabling better decision-making.
   - **Importance**: User-friendly interfaces help stakeholders engage with the system and understand its recommendations.
5. **Integration with Renewable Energy Sources**: Smart EMS must be designed to accommodate variable energy generation from renewable sources, such as solar and wind, ensuring reliable energy supply.
   - **Importance**: Effective integration helps balance the energy mix and reduces reliance on fossil fuels.

Challenges in Designing Smart EMS:

- **Data Privacy and Security**: Ensuring the security of sensitive data collected from users and systems is critical in maintaining trust and compliance with regulations.
- **Interoperability**: Integrating various devices, systems, and protocols from different manufacturers can be challenging, requiring standardized communication frameworks.
- **Scalability**: As energy demand grows, smart EMS must be scalable to accommodate increasing data volumes and system complexities.

11.2 Role of AI in Managing Renewable and Conventional Energy Mix

The integration of AI into energy management systems plays a vital role in balancing the renewable and conventional energy mix. AI enhances decision-making processes and operational efficiency through predictive analytics and optimization techniques.

Key Roles of AI:

1. **Predictive Analytics for Demand Forecasting**: AI algorithms analyze historical energy consumption data and external factors (such as weather patterns) to accurately predict future energy demand.

  - **Benefits:** Improved demand forecasting allows for better planning and scheduling of energy resources, minimizing reliance on peaking power plants.

2. **Dynamic Resource Allocation:** AI enables dynamic adjustments to energy generation and consumption strategies, optimizing the mix of renewable and conventional sources based on real-time data.
   - **Example:** AI systems can prioritize renewable generation when available, switching to conventional sources only when needed to meet demand.
3. **Energy Storage Management:** AI-driven systems optimize the operation of energy storage solutions (like batteries) by predicting when to charge or discharge based on demand and generation forecasts.
   - **Benefits:** Effective energy storage management enhances grid reliability and supports renewable energy integration.
4. **Demand Response Programs:** AI facilitates demand response initiatives by analyzing user consumption patterns and encouraging consumers to shift their usage during peak periods.
   - **Benefits:** By incentivizing users to adjust their consumption, AI helps flatten demand peaks and reduce stress on the grid.
5. **Grid Stability and Reliability:** AI algorithms monitor grid conditions and make real-time adjustments to maintain voltage and frequency stability, improving overall reliability.
   - **Techniques:** Machine learning models can detect anomalies and predict potential outages, allowing for proactive measures to maintain grid stability.

Example of AI in Action:

- **Smart Grid Applications:** AI algorithms are employed in smart grids to manage energy flows from various sources, ensuring optimal utilization of available resources while maintaining system reliability.

11.3 Case Studies in Smart Grid Integration

Real-world case studies illustrate the successful implementation of AI-driven energy management systems and their impact on smart grid integration. These examples demonstrate the effectiveness of advanced technologies in enhancing operational efficiency, reliability, and sustainability.

Case Study 1: Smart Home Energy Management Systems

In a residential community, an AI-driven smart home energy management system was implemented to optimize energy consumption. The system utilized machine learning algorithms to analyze historical usage data and real-time inputs from smart meters. By predicting peak usage times and adjusting energy consumption accordingly, the system reduced energy bills by 20% while increasing the use of renewable energy sources.

Case Study 2: Commercial Energy Management

A large commercial building implemented a smart EMS that integrated AI for energy monitoring and management. The system analyzed data from HVAC, lighting, and electrical systems to identify inefficiencies. AI algorithms provided recommendations for optimizing energy usage, resulting in a 30% reduction in energy costs and significant improvements in overall building performance.

Case Study 3: Utility-Scale Renewable Integration

A utility company adopted an AI-driven energy management system to integrate a mix of renewable and conventional energy sources. The system utilized predictive analytics to forecast energy generation from solar and wind while optimizing the dispatch of conventional power plants. As a result, the utility achieved a 15% increase in renewable energy utilization and enhanced grid reliability.

CHAPTER TWELVE

Emerging Trends in Machine Learning for Power Electronics

As technology evolves, the intersection of machine learning (ML) and power electronics is experiencing rapid innovation. This chapter explores emerging trends that are shaping the future of power electronics, including the role of AI in cybersecurity for renewable energy grids, advances in real-time analytics and edge computing, and anticipated future trends in the integration of power electronics and machine learning.

12.1 AI for Cybersecurity in Renewable Energy Grids

The increasing complexity of renewable energy grids, combined with their reliance on interconnected devices and digital systems, has raised significant cybersecurity concerns. As cyber threats become more sophisticated, integrating artificial intelligence into cybersecurity measures is critical for protecting energy infrastructure.

Key Aspects of AI-Driven Cybersecurity:

1. **Threat Detection and Response**: AI algorithms can analyze vast amounts of data from network traffic and system logs to identify anomalies that may indicate potential cyberattacks. Machine learning models can be trained to detect patterns associated with known threats and adapt to new ones.
    - **Techniques**: Techniques such as supervised learning can be employed to classify network behaviors and flag suspicious activities in real time.
2. **Predictive Analytics**: AI systems can forecast potential vulnerabilities in the grid infrastructure based on historical data, enabling proactive measures to be taken before an attack occurs.
    - **Importance**: Predictive analytics help in prioritizing security resources and implementing patches or updates to vulnerable systems.
3. **Incident Response Automation**: AI can facilitate automated responses to detected threats, reducing response times and minimizing damage. Automated systems can isolate compromised components and initiate recovery protocols.
    - **Example**: AI-driven systems can automatically adjust grid operations in response to cyber threats, ensuring continued service while addressing vulnerabilities.
4. **Enhanced Security Protocols**: Machine learning can assist in developing advanced security protocols that evolve with emerging threats, adapting to changing attack vectors and techniques.

- **Importance**: Continuous learning allows systems to strengthen defenses based on real-time data and trends in cyber threats.

Real-World Implications:

- Implementing AI for cybersecurity in renewable energy grids is essential for safeguarding critical infrastructure, ensuring reliable energy delivery, and protecting sensitive data from breaches.

12.2 Advances in Real-Time Analytics and Edge Computing

The rise of real-time analytics and edge computing has transformed the way data is processed and analyzed in power electronics. These technologies enable faster decision-making and improved operational efficiency in energy systems.

Key Advances:

1. **Real-Time Data Processing**: The ability to analyze data as it is generated allows for immediate insights and actions, enhancing system responsiveness and performance.
   - **Applications**: Real-time analytics can optimize energy dispatch, improve fault detection, and enable demand response strategies in real time.
2. **Edge Computing**: By processing data closer to the source (e.g., at the edge of the network), edge computing reduces latency and bandwidth requirements. This is particularly beneficial in distributed energy systems where data from multiple sources must be managed efficiently.
   - **Benefits**: Edge computing enhances the scalability of energy management systems, reduces reliance on centralized data centers, and improves overall system resilience.
3. **Integration with IoT Devices**: The proliferation of Internet of Things (IoT) devices in energy systems enables more granular data collection and analysis. Real-time analytics can leverage data from these devices to optimize operations and enhance decision-making.
   - **Example**: Smart meters and sensors can provide real-time feedback on energy consumption and generation, allowing for immediate adjustments to energy management strategies.
4. **Machine Learning at the Edge**: Deploying machine learning algorithms at the edge allows for localized decision-making and reduces the need for constant communication with central servers. This is crucial for applications requiring rapid responses, such as fault detection and system control.
   - **Importance**: Edge ML models can operate autonomously, enhancing reliability and reducing the risks associated with communication failures.

12.3 Future Trends in Power Electronics and ML Integration

As the field of power electronics continues to evolve, several key trends are emerging in the integration of machine learning technologies:

1. **Increased Adoption of Digital Twins:** Digital twin technology involves creating a virtual replica of physical systems, allowing for real-time monitoring and predictive analytics. The integration of machine learning can enhance the accuracy and effectiveness of digital twins in optimizing power electronics systems.

    ◦ **Applications:** Digital twins can be used for simulating system behavior under different scenarios, aiding in design, testing, and predictive maintenance.

2. **AI-Powered Optimization Algorithms:** Future developments will see the increased use of AI algorithms for optimizing power converter operations and energy dispatch strategies. Techniques such as genetic algorithms, reinforcement learning, and other advanced optimization methods will become standard in power electronics applications.

    ◦ **Importance:** These algorithms can lead to improved energy efficiency, reduced operational costs, and enhanced system reliability.

3. **Decentralized Energy Systems:** The trend towards decentralized energy generation (e.g., microgrids, community solar projects) will drive the need for sophisticated machine learning algorithms to manage complex interactions between local energy resources, storage, and consumption.

    ◦ **Benefits:** Machine learning will facilitate real-time optimization of energy flows and enhance the stability of decentralized systems.

4. **Integration of Renewable Energy Sources:** As the share of renewables in the energy mix increases, machine learning will play a critical role in managing the variability and uncertainty associated with these sources. AI-driven forecasting models and control strategies will enhance the integration of renewables into existing power systems.

    ◦ **Example:** Advanced forecasting techniques using machine learning can improve grid reliability by accurately predicting renewable generation patterns.

5. **Sustainability and Energy Efficiency:** Future trends will focus on leveraging machine learning to promote sustainability and improve energy efficiency in power electronic systems. AI can be used to analyze energy usage patterns and identify opportunities for optimization and waste reduction.

    ◦ **Importance:** Emphasizing sustainability will align with global efforts to reduce carbon emissions and transition to cleaner energy sources.

CHAPTER THIRTEEN

Case Studies and Real-World Applications

As machine learning (ML) continues to advance, its applications in renewable energy systems, particularly solar, wind, and hybrid setups, are becoming increasingly prevalent. This section explores various case studies that illustrate how ML has been effectively implemented in these sectors, discusses the industrial adoption of these technologies along with practical challenges, and concludes with the lessons learned and future directions for ML applications in energy systems.

13.1 Case Studies of ML Applications in Solar, Wind, and Hybrid Systems

1. **Solar Energy Management**
    - **Case Study**: A solar farm in California implemented an ML-driven predictive maintenance system to monitor the health of its photovoltaic (PV) panels. Using real-time data from sensors and historical performance metrics, the system predicts potential failures before they occur.
    - **Outcomes**: The application of machine learning reduced maintenance costs by 25% and improved overall energy production by 10% by minimizing downtime through timely interventions.
2. **Wind Energy Optimization**
    - **Case Study**: A leading wind energy company utilized machine learning algorithms to optimize turbine performance. The ML models analyzed wind speed, direction, and turbine output data to fine-tune turbine settings in real-time.
    - **Outcomes**: This resulted in a 15% increase in energy capture during peak wind conditions and a reduction in mechanical wear and tear, leading to lower operational costs.
3. **Hybrid Renewable Systems**
    - **Case Study**: In a hybrid renewable energy project combining solar and wind, ML algorithms were employed to optimize energy dispatch between the two sources. The system used historical data to forecast generation patterns and load demands.
    - **Outcomes**: This integration led to improved energy efficiency and a reduction in reliance on diesel generators, decreasing carbon emissions by 30% and significantly lowering operational costs.

13.2 Industrial Adoption and Practical Challenges

While the potential benefits of machine learning in renewable energy systems are significant, various challenges have emerged in the industrial adoption of these technologies:

1. **Data Quality and Availability**:

- **Challenge**: Many renewable energy projects struggle with insufficient or low-quality data, which hampers the effectiveness of ML algorithms. Inconsistent data collection methods and lack of standardized protocols can lead to unreliable insights.
- **Solution**: Investing in robust data collection infrastructure and adopting standard protocols can improve data quality and enable better machine learning applications.

2. **Integration with Existing Systems**:

   - **Challenge**: The integration of ML models into existing energy management systems can be complex and costly. Legacy systems may not be compatible with modern ML tools, leading to potential disruptions.
   - **Solution**: Developing modular ML solutions that can be incrementally integrated into existing systems can help mitigate these challenges.

3. **Skill Gap**:

   - **Challenge**: There is often a lack of expertise in both machine learning and renewable energy technologies, which can hinder successful implementation.
   - **Solution**: Training programs and interdisciplinary collaboration can bridge the skill gap, empowering teams to leverage ML effectively.

4. **Regulatory and Compliance Issues**:

   - **Challenge**: The energy sector is heavily regulated, and the use of AI and ML technologies must comply with various regulations and standards, which can slow down innovation.
   - **Solution**: Engaging with regulatory bodies early in the development process can help ensure compliance while fostering innovation.

13.3 Lessons Learned and Future Directions

1. **Importance of Collaboration**:

   - **Lesson Learned**: Successful ML applications in renewable energy often require collaboration among stakeholders, including energy producers, technology developers, and data scientists. Interdisciplinary teams can drive innovation and ensure that solutions are practical and effective.

2. **Continuous Improvement**:

   - **Lesson Learned**: Machine learning models require ongoing training and refinement based on new data and changing conditions. Organizations should adopt a culture of continuous improvement to maximize the benefits of ML.

3. **Focus on Scalability**:

   - **Lesson Learned**: Developing scalable solutions is crucial for widespread adoption. ML applications should be designed to adapt to various energy systems and operational scales.

4. **Future Directions**:

- **Enhanced Algorithms**: The development of more sophisticated ML algorithms, such as deep learning and reinforcement learning, holds promise for improving the accuracy and reliability of energy forecasting and optimization.
- **Edge Computing**: The integration of edge computing with machine learning will enable real-time processing and decision-making, enhancing responsiveness in dynamic energy environments.
- **Decentralized Energy Solutions**: As decentralized energy systems become more prevalent, machine learning will play a critical role in managing distributed energy resources and optimizing local energy use.
- **Sustainability and Resilience**: Future ML applications will increasingly focus on enhancing the sustainability and resilience of energy systems, helping to mitigate the impacts of climate change and promote energy security.

CHAPTER FOURTEEN

Future Directions and Challenges

As the integration of machine learning and artificial intelligence (AI) into energy systems continues to expand, it is essential to address the future directions and challenges that accompany this evolution. This section explores ethical considerations in AI for energy systems, regulatory challenges in renewable energy integration, and pathways for research and development.

Ethical Considerations in AI for Energy Systems

The deployment of AI technologies in energy systems raises several ethical considerations that must be addressed to ensure responsible use and societal acceptance:

1. **Transparency and Accountability**:
    - **Concern**: AI systems, particularly those employing deep learning techniques, can often operate as "black boxes," making it difficult to understand how decisions are made. This lack of transparency can lead to mistrust among stakeholders and users.
    - **Solution**: Developing interpretable AI models and establishing clear accountability frameworks can help demystify AI decision-making processes and foster trust among users.
2. **Bias and Fairness**:
    - **Concern**: AI algorithms can inadvertently perpetuate existing biases present in training data, leading to unfair outcomes. This is particularly critical in energy systems where equitable access to resources and services is paramount.
    - **Solution**: Implementing fairness-aware algorithms and regularly auditing AI systems for biases can help mitigate these issues, ensuring that energy services are accessible and equitable for all communities.
3. **Data Privacy and Security**:
    - **Concern**: The use of large datasets in AI applications raises concerns about data privacy and security. Sensitive information about energy consumption patterns could be misused or accessed by unauthorized parties.
    - **Solution**: Adopting robust data governance frameworks and employing techniques such as data anonymization can help protect user privacy while still enabling valuable insights.
4. **Environmental Impact**:
    - **Concern**: The environmental impact of AI technologies, particularly in terms of energy consumption for data processing and model training, must be considered. AI applications should not undermine sustainability goals.
    - **Solution**: Striving for energy-efficient algorithms and optimizing the computational resources used in AI applications can help minimize their environmental footprint.

Regulatory Challenges in Renewable Energy Integration

As renewable energy systems become more prevalent, various regulatory challenges must be navigated to facilitate their integration:

1. **Inconsistent Regulations:**

    ◦ **Challenge:** Regulatory frameworks for renewable energy often vary significantly across regions and jurisdictions, creating confusion and hindering the deployment of innovative technologies.
    ◦ **Solution:** Establishing standardized regulations that promote consistency across regions can facilitate smoother integration and innovation in renewable energy technologies.

2. **Grid Interconnection Standards:**

    ◦ **Challenge:** The integration of distributed energy resources (DERs) into existing grids presents technical challenges related to interconnection standards and grid stability.
    ◦ **Solution:** Developing clear interconnection standards and guidelines that address the unique characteristics of renewable energy sources can enhance grid reliability and safety.

3. **Incentives and Support Mechanisms:**

    ◦ **Challenge:** The lack of adequate incentives and support mechanisms for renewable energy adoption can slow progress in deploying AI and machine learning technologies.
    ◦ **Solution:** Policymakers should consider implementing incentives, grants, and funding mechanisms to encourage investment in renewable energy projects that leverage AI technologies.

4. **Data Sharing and Access:**

    ◦ **Challenge:** Regulatory barriers related to data sharing can impede the development of effective AI applications in energy systems, as collaboration and access to data are crucial for training algorithms.
    ◦ **Solution:** Encouraging open data initiatives and establishing partnerships among public and private sectors can promote data sharing while ensuring compliance with privacy regulations.

Pathways for Research and Development

To address the challenges and maximize the potential of AI in energy systems, several pathways for research and development should be pursued:

1. **Interdisciplinary Research:**

    ◦ **Focus:** Encouraging interdisciplinary collaboration between energy scientists, data scientists, and social scientists can lead to holistic approaches that address technical, ethical, and societal challenges in AI applications.
    ◦ **Benefits:** This collaboration can foster innovative solutions that are technically sound while being socially responsible and ethically grounded.

2. **Advanced AI Techniques:**

    ◦ **Focus:** Research into advanced AI techniques, such as reinforcement learning, deep learning, and federated learning, can enhance the capability of AI systems in predicting energy consumption patterns, optimizing

operations, and improving decision-making processes.
- **Benefits**: These techniques can lead to more accurate forecasting, efficient energy management, and enhanced system reliability.

3. **Pilot Projects and Prototyping**:

    - **Focus**: Developing pilot projects and prototypes to test AI applications in real-world settings can provide valuable insights into their effectiveness and scalability.
    - **Benefits**: These projects can help identify practical challenges, refine algorithms, and validate the benefits of AI in energy systems.

4. **Public Engagement and Education**:

    - **Focus**: Raising public awareness and understanding of AI technologies in energy systems is crucial for gaining societal acceptance and support.
    - **Benefits**: Educational initiatives can empower stakeholders to engage with AI technologies actively and contribute to discussions about ethical and regulatory considerations.

www.ingramcontent.com/pod-product-compliance
Lightning Source LLC
LaVergne TN
LVHW070942160826
845679LV00022B/1889

* 9 7 9 8 8 9 6 1 0 1 8 5 7 *